'I can't beli
she said, he
short spurts
relieved to see anyone in my life.

He managed a wry smile. 'Me, too. I felt I had to come and make sure that you were safe.'

A little glow started up inside her. 'So you came here especially to make sure that I was all right?' She pulled in a deep breath. 'I'm so relieved that's all over.'

'So am I.' Rhys put his arms around her, gathering her up, and she went into his embrace, feeling that for once the world was spinning properly on its axis.

Abby shuddered. 'It feels as though I've been working my way through one long nightmare,' she said. 'Is it finally over?'

He stroked her hair, his other arm circling her and keeping her close to him. Her whole body warmed at his touch. 'It's over,' he said. 'Only, perhaps another dream is just beginning…'

When **Joanna Neil** discovered Mills & Boon®, her life-long addiction to reading crystallised into an exciting new career writing Medical Romance™. Her characters are probably the outcome of her varied lifestyle, which includes working as a clerk, typist, nurse and infant teacher. She enjoys dressmaking and cooking at her Leicestershire home. Her family includes a husband, son and daughter, an exuberant yellow Labrador and two slightly crazed cockatiels. She currently works with a team of tutors at her local education centre, to provide creative writing workshops for people interested in exploring their own writing ambitions.

Recent titles by the same author:

THE LONDON CONSULTANT'S RESCUE

BY

JOANNA NEIL

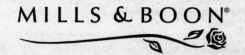

MILLS & BOON®

All the characters in this book have no existence outside the imagination of the author, and have no relation whatsoever to anyone bearing the same name or names. They are not even distantly inspired by any individual known or unknown to the author, and all the incidents are pure invention.

First published in Great Britain 2006
Paperback edition 2007
Harlequin Mills & Boon Limited,
Eton House, 18-24 Paradise Road, Richmond, Surrey TW9 1SR

© Joanna Neil 2006

ISBN-13: 978 0 263 85221 9
ISBN-10:   0 263 85221 0

Set in Times Roman 10½ on 13 pt
03-0207-46881

Printed and bound in Spain
by Litografia Rosés, S.A., Barcelona

THE LONDON CONSULTANT'S RESCUE

CHAPTER ONE

'THIS is all a bit unsettling, isn't it? Do you think you'll be able to cope with everything all right?' Emma's mother sent her a concerned look. 'I'm surprised they changed your schedule at such short notice.'

Emma swallowed the last dregs of her coffee and reluctantly put her cup back down on the table.

'I'll be OK, Mum. Most doctors working in our A and E department get to do a stint with the air ambulance at some point but you're quite right, it was a sudden change of plan. I wasn't expecting to go out with them for a few months yet, but now that the registrar's fallen ill, things have had to be hastily rearranged. The end result is that I'm going to be taking his place for a while. He's not too happy about it—he wants to specialise in working with the rescue service and he was bitterly disappointed at not to be able to go on with things as arranged.'

She hesitated, and then added, 'I dare say it will be good experience for me, though. It was unexpected, and I'm a bit at sixes and sevens just now, but I'm sure I'll manage.'

Emma hunted around for her medical bag and started to throw in a few extra items, a roll of gauze and a pair of sharp scissors among them.

Her mother was still worried. 'Didn't I hear that Rhys Benton was working with the helicopter emergency service?' She glanced towards the hallway as though she was half-afraid that Emma's father would come downstairs and hear their conversation. She lowered her voice. 'Are you likely to run into him at some point?'

Emma frowned. She had wondered about that herself. 'It's true that he's with the air ambulance, but he's always worked a different shift pattern from me. Our paths haven't crossed so far, and I've been with A and E for more than a year now.'

She sent her mother a quick smile. 'Actually, I've already met the doctor in charge, so at least I know that we'll get on well together. Colin's an easygoing sort of fellow. He's married, and his wife has just had their first baby.'

She zipped up her medical bag and then scooped up her purse and car keys. 'I suppose I'd better go. I want to get there early for my first day.' She gave her mother an affectionate hug. 'Thanks for breakfast, Mum. Say goodbye to Dad for me, will you? I hope he's going to be feeling a bit better soon. Perhaps you and he could come over to my place for a meal when he's feeling more up to it?'

Her mother nodded. 'I'll look forward to it. I'm sure your dad's just a bit overtired, and that's why he's under the weather. He's been working hard, trying to get this new business venture off the ground, and it's all been a bit of a strain for him, given everything that he's gone through in the past.'

'I know, but I'm sure things will work out for him this time.' They had to. Emma's green eyes clouded as she thought about the way her father's dreams had collapsed. If he had to suffer any more setbacks, he would surely be a broken man.

Her mother returned the embrace, and after another minute or two Emma set off for the hospital.

It was only a short tube ride away and a little while later she was in the hospital lift, heading for the top floor of the building where the air ambulance crew had their headquarters.

They were based in a block a short distance from the helipad, in a set of rooms that was stocked with up-to-the-minute equipment, with everything on hand for emergencies and communications.

As Emma entered, she saw a group of men gathered around a table, talking to one another while they checked the navigation system or monitored the computer screens. One of them, the tallest, looked up as she approached, and it seemed as though he was about to greet her, but then the smile froze on his face.

Emma stared at him in return and came to a sudden halt, her mouth opening and closing in dismay. It wasn't possible, was it? How could this be happening to her? Hadn't she assured her mother only a short time ago that there was absolutely no chance of her running into Rhys Benton…? And yet now he was here straightening up, his firmly muscled body taut like a coiled spring.

He was also frowning, his gaze moving slowly over her, taking in the mass of chestnut curls that framed her face and drifted down in wild disarray to brush her shoulders. His glance shifted to trail over her slender length and then returned to rest in scarcely veiled astonishment on her face once more.

'Emma? What are you doing here?' Rhys's voice was gravel deep, just as she remembered, cutting into her mesmerised thoughts, disturbing her fragile peace of mind.

For a long moment her voice seemed to have deserted her, and all she could think was that she might have asked him the very same question. He was the last person she had expected to come across, but here he was, as large as life, long-limbed, lean and superbly fit, his features clean cut, his jaw line angular and his whole appearance heartrendingly easy on the eye.

All the old feelings of aching loss and bitter disillusionment shimmered through her and she drew in a deep, shuddery breath. She had hoped that all these emotions had long since been well and truly buried, and it hurt to realise that they were there in full force once more, as though time had stood still.

Emma could see that he was still waiting for an answer. She said carefully, 'Our registrar has gone down with some kind of bug, so I'm here in his place. I'm supposed to work alongside the crew as a trainee.' Under his unblinking stare, her gaze faltered. 'I thought Colin would be here. I was told to report to him.'

Rhys shook his head. 'He's away on paternity leave just now.'

'Oh, I see.' She absorbed that. 'But he'll be back in a week or so, won't he?' she asked hopefully, her head lifting a fraction.

'I'm afraid not. He's changed shifts, so that he can be with his family more. I've been asked to take over as the consultant in charge during daylight hours.'

'Oh.' Her tone was flat, and it occurred to her that she ought to have tried to disguise her disappointment. Maybe he had missed it, though, because his attention shifted to a sheaf of papers that were clamped to his clipboard and he was frowning again. Emma guessed that he was checking what she had just said. It didn't come as any surprise that he was none too pleased to have her arrive there as a substitute for the registrar.

It seemed, though, that he must have realised that it was too late now to do anything about it. After a moment he said briskly, 'I expect you already know Martin.' He glanced towards the paramedic.

She nodded. 'Yes, we've met.'

Martin gave her a quick smile, but Rhys was already moving on. 'And this is James, our pilot, and Chris, the copilot.' He waved a hand in the direction of the two men. 'I imagine you must know them, too.'

'Yes.' She smiled their way briefly, and they responded in similar fashion, though there was a curious glint in James's eyes, as though he sensed a source of friction between Emma and Rhys.

'Good.' The preliminaries over, Rhys's gaze

narrowed on her once more, and he said, 'You'll need to kit yourself out with a uniform.' He indicated a cupboard at the far side of the room. 'Rummage through the pile in there. There should be one in your size, and you can change in the dressing room.'

The atmosphere between them was decidedly tense, impenetrable, like a dark cloud barrier, and Emma didn't wait to be told any more. She was glad of the excuse to escape, and hurried away to get changed into the bright outfit worn by the emergency service. She fretted in silence over the sudden change in circumstances, her heart still thumping erratically from the shock of seeing him here.

A few minutes later she was ready, but as she went to join the others she saw that the whole setup had changed. The crew was gearing up, and already the pilot and copilot were heading out towards the helipad. No one had told her that she needed to hurry, and she couldn't help wondering whether they would have gone without her if she hadn't been ready.

'We've had a call out to a boating accident on the Thames,' Rhys said, his tone curt. 'Get your stuff together and we'll be on our way.'

A little while later she settled herself beside him in the helicopter. The pilot already had the engine running, getting ready for take-off. Strapping herself into her seat, she looked around and saw that there was room for two patients to be brought in by stretcher and flown back to safety.

'What happened? Do you know the details?' she asked Rhys.

'Only that two boats collided. There were a few casualties, but it looks as though we're going to be dealing with a head injury and a fracture of some sort.'

'It's a bit early in the day for that sort of accident, isn't it?'

'Not really. It's the holiday season, and I expect people get out onto the water just as soon as they can. You get a lot of inexperienced boaters taking to the water whenever the weather is fine.'

Emma subsided into silence as the helicopter took to the air. It was a strange sensation, being lifted up into the skies, and it wasn't one that she had experienced before in quite this form. Soon, though, she adjusted to the situation, and she looked down at the landscape beneath her. She could see for miles around, and it was a heady sensation. Sunlight shone down on the river, making it look like a ribbon of glass, reflecting the buildings along its course, and skyscrapers rose majestically across the city of London so that she could pinpoint various landmarks along the way.

Rhys said, 'Do your parents still live on the North Downs? I know there was some talk of them moving away.'

She grimaced. Why had he brought that up? Didn't he know how much it had grieved her parents to leave the family home? They had brought up their daughters there and they had cherished the fresh air of the countryside, loved the freedom of having meadowland all around. Uprooting themselves had been almost more than they had been able to bear.

Emma didn't tell him any of that, though. Instead, she said, 'They bought a smaller place, closer to the City, so that it would be easier for them to commute. My dad put some money from the sale into property and spent some time refurbishing the building so that he could let it out as flats.' It was one way that he was trying to recoup his income.

'I heard that he had tried something of the sort. How have things worked out for him?'

She said cautiously, 'It's taken a while, but he's beginning to make some headway. There were a few setbacks along the way, with disruptions with the builders and so on, but things are beginning to fall into place.' That was a hefty understatement. Her father had struggled all the way after his business had collapsed, and it had seemed as though nothing had gone right with the next venture he had taken on.

She felt uncomfortable, talking about her father with Rhys of all people, and by way of a change of subject she asked, 'What about your parents? Do they still live up at the hall?'

'They do. It's been in the family for generations, so I doubt they would willingly sell up.'

No, she could understand that. The hall was surrounded by acres of land, and the house itself nestled into a hillside, a picturesque building of weathered yellow stone set against a backdrop of trees and flowering shrubs. Coming from the same village as Rhys, Emma had been a visitor to the hall on a number of occasions. His parents often held open house, hosting fêtes and charity sales in the grounds, and she had come to know him and his family well over the years.

All the easy familiarity that passed between them had come to a sudden stop, though, after the awful accident at her father's restaurant. Nothing had been the same since then, and that was hardly surprising, given that Rhys's sister had been hurt that day. What should have been a pleasant meeting for lunch with a friend after a morning's shopping had turned into something too dreadful to contemplate.

She glanced up at him now, and saw that his expression was strained. Was he remembering, just as she had done? He had been careful not to make any mention of it up to now, but they both knew that what had happened two years ago was there between them, stinging like an open wound.

'How is your sister?' she asked in an apprehensive tone. 'I tried to keep in touch with her, but she moved house and I haven't been able to contact her in a long while.'

He grimaced. 'I think she's recovered well enough from the physical wounds—they were the least of her problems, after all—but I wouldn't say that she was all right by a long way. The mental scars will take much longer to heal.'

'I'm sorry.'

He nodded, but didn't say any more.

'OK, folks. This must be the place.' The pilot's voice reached them suddenly and jolted them back to the present. 'There's quite a crowd gathered down there, and it looks as though the press have arrived already. I can see someone with a camera, taking pictures. I guess the police must have their hands full.'

Emma's glance took in the curving stretch of the River Thames as the helicopter descended and settled onto firm ground once more. She saw that they had landed some distance from a wharf where boats were moored, bobbing gently on the water as they were tossed by a slight breeze.

Rhys and Martin were already on the move, exiting the helicopter. Emma hesitated for a moment, still finding her feet after the unaccustomed flight, but then she quickly followed suit, preparing to jump down from the belly of the aircraft. Rhys put out an arm to steady her and, much as she was wary of accepting his help, she was thankful for that gesture of support.

'Are you OK?' he asked.

She nodded. 'I'm fine, thanks,' she mumbled. She wasn't, though, not by a long way. His strong fingers gripped hers and a swift current of electricity rippled through her hand and along her arm and jerked her out of her safe cocoon of isolation. She didn't want to acknowledge that he had any kind of effect on her at all.

He looked at her quizzically for a second or two, and then released her, turning away and heading over to the riverside where people were assembled at the water's edge. She followed him, forcing herself to breathe deeply in order to calm herself.

As they approached a concrete slipway, and it was plain to see that there had been some kind of collision.

Two small motorboats had been pulled up out of the water onto the landing stage, and it was clear that they were badly damaged.

Debris floated on the water, washing away downstream, and Emma saw that there were shifting sandbanks hugging the bend of the river, exposed by the low water level.

'What happened here?' Rhys went to talk to a paramedic from the ambulance that was already at the scene, and together they hurried to where a man and boy lay injured on the slipway. At the same time Emma noticed that a man and a woman were being wheeled to the vehicle, in readiness for their journey to the nearest hospital.

'As far as I can make out, the couple in the first boat misjudged the curve in the river and took the bend too wide and too fast. The man in the other boat was coming in the opposite direction and manoeuvred to avoid being hit, but swerved into the side of the slipway. He was thrown overboard and hit his head on the side of the concrete ramp as he went into the water. His son, Matthew, toppled over with some force and fell against the side of the boat. Apparently, he put his arm out to save himself and it looks as though he's ended up with a broken bone.'

Rhys winced. 'Ouch. That sounds nasty. Are they both conscious?'

'The boy is. The father has a GCS score of 8 and his condition seems to be deteriorating. He was pulled out of the water only just in time—he very nearly drowned.'

'He was wearing a life jacket, wasn't he?' Rhys was already bending to examine the man.

'Yes but it wasn't inflated properly—either that or there was a tear in it somewhere.'

Emma went with Martin to assess the boy's condition.

'Hello, Matthew,' she said, kneeling down beside him and greeting him with a smile. 'I'm Emma—I'm a doctor, and this is Martin, a paramedic. We've come to take you and your dad to hospital, but first I want to take a look at your arm, and then we'll see if we can make you feel a little more comfortable. Is that all right with you?'

Matthew didn't look too sure about that, but he gave a very faint nod. He was about seven years old, fair-haired and pale-looking, and although the paramedics had already treated him initially, Emma was worried about him. His face was tearstained, and he was shocked and obviously distressed about his father.

'Are you from the helicopter?' he asked, looking from one to the other.

'That's right…we are,' Emma answered. 'Do you fancy a ride in it?'

He nodded, looking at her with wide-eyed uncertainty. 'With my dad as well?' He glanced at his father, lying just a short distance away from them.

'Oh, yes. Definitely with your dad.'

The boy appeared to relax a little at that, and once Emma had managed to gain his confidence sufficiently she checked his injured upper arm. It was a nasty break, a displaced and angulated fracture near the elbow, and straight away she could see that more problems were developing.

Turning to Martin, she said softly, 'There's a lot of swelling, and there must have been considerable bleeding into the tissues. I'm afraid there may have been damage to the brachial artery. The whole area is very tense around the break, and even with the painkilling medication that he's been given he's having difficulty contracting the muscles. I'm afraid he's suffering from compartment syndrome. We need to get him to Theatre fast.'

Martin recorded the results as Emma continued to test the distal pulses and check for sensation. 'I'll immobilise the arm for now,' he said, 'and monitor his pulse and blood pressure.' He looked at Matthew. 'As soon as I've done that, I'll put the blanket back around you, because we have to do our best to keep you warm.'

Emma nodded agreement, and then smiled at the boy once more. 'I have something for you,' she told him. Delving into her medical bag, she brought out a teddy-bear sticker and colouring sheet, along with a 'brave boy' certificate. 'You've been such a good patient—the best—so these are for you, though you'll probably need to learn to colour with your other hand.'

Matthew managed a faint lift at the corners of his mouth, and then he studied the certificate with interest.

Emma spoke quietly to Martin. 'We'll top up his pain relief, and on our way back to the hospital I'll refer him to the orthopaedic surgeon for open reduction and internal fixation.' She hesitated momentarily. 'I should go and see if Rhys needs any help.'

'That's OK. I can manage here.'

She hurried to Rhys's side and discovered that he was deeply concerned about his patient. He had intubated Matthew's father so that his airway was protected, and he was being given oxygen.

'He has a fractured skull,' Rhys explained. 'He's been seizing and I've given him diazepam to control the fits, but we need to take measures to prevent any more. He's slipping more deeply into unconsciousness, and his pupils are dilating.'

Emma sucked in her breath. That was a sure sign of intracranial pressure, and it probably meant that there must be a haematoma, a blood clot, building up inside his skull. Things weren't looking good for the man.

'Do you want me to start an infusion of phenytoin to prevent any more fits?' she asked.

'Yes. I'm going to give him a bolus of intravenous mannitol to lower the intracranial pressure and hopefully buy us a little time, but we need to get him out of here, fast.'

Emma understood that. It was imperative that the patient went for surgery to drain the haematoma before any more damage occurred.

She started the intravenous infusion and was about to get to her feet once more when she was almost blinded by a sudden flash of bright light.

'I know you from somewhere, don't I?' a man said, and as her vision cleared she looked up and saw that he was adjusting the setting of his camera. 'Didn't we meet up at another incident some time ago?' he went on. 'I don't think you were wearing a medic's outfit then, though.' He frowned, as though he was trying to remember, and then he stared at her once more and his face lit up with a rush of realisation. 'I know where it was… There was a fire, wasn't there…and an explosion? Wasn't it your father's restaurant that went up in flames?'

Emma did her best to shield her patient with her body. He didn't need prying eyes looking at him in his vulnerable state. At the same time a hollow feeling invaded her stomach and she felt a shiver run through her body, a reaction to the second shock of the day that she'd had to endure.

She hadn't needed the journalist's reminder. She recognised him all too well, and meeting up with him this way was more than she could handle right now.

'We're busy here,' she said. 'I don't have time to stop and talk to you.'

He didn't seem at all deterred by her comment, and raised his camera once more. 'It was a gas cylinder that did the damage, wasn't it? Something about a back-up for the outdoor barbecues that your father used to put on for the customers. Only it was stored in the wrong place, as I recall.'

Rhys intervened. 'We have a job to do,' he said in a brusque tone. 'There are injured people here and they need our attention. Don't take any more photos, and clear the way.'

Grim-faced, he brushed past the man, forcing him to move to one side to let them pass. Then he manoeuvred his patient off the slipway, directing the stretcher trolley towards the waiting helicopter.

Emma followed with Matthew and Martin. The experience had alarmed and thoroughly unsettled her. Did the journalist really think she needed any reminders of that awful day when her world had turned upside down?

'Have you met him before?' Martin asked, and she nodded.

'Unfortunately, yes, I have.'

Her thoughts were drowned out. The pilot had the helicopter's engine turning over, ready for take-off as soon as they gave the word, and Emma looked down at seven-year-old Matthew once more and slowly came to her senses. Why was she worrying about a journalist from her past when she had to get this little boy and his father to hospital? Their lives were more important than her battered feelings. Nothing else mattered, did it?

They settled their patients inside the helicopter and checked the equipment and the drips, making sure that all was well. When they had finished and were ready to go, she glanced across at Rhys.

His expression was bleak and his mouth was set in a taut line. She guessed that he must be recalling how his sister had been hurt that day at the restaurant. He didn't need to say anything... Emma could almost read his thoughts, and she understood perfectly well how he must feel.

'I'm sorry that we had to run into that journalist,' she

said. 'He seemed to be all over us on the night of the explosion, and it was the same today. As soon as I saw him I was worried. He exaggerated what happened at the restaurant in his article back then, and I just wonder what kind of story he's going to write about this incident. He can't make too much of a simple boating accident, can he?'

'He didn't put anything in print that could be disputed, did he?' Rhys's eyes were dark, his features etched with brooding intensity. 'He was right about the gas cylinder. It was in the wrong place and when it exploded it caused a lot of damage.'

'But he made it sound as though my father was neg-ligent…as though everything that happened was his fault…'

'I don't see that you can take him to task over that. He was pointing out the facts and, whether you like it or not, ultimately your father was responsible for what happened.'

She sucked in an anguished breath. 'But he said that he had stored the cylinder properly, well away from any risk of harm, and I believe him. He would never do anything to jeopardise people's safety. He was never charged with negligence.'

'Because nothing could be proved. Anyway, I'm sure he wouldn't have wanted anyone to be hurt, but that wasn't how things turned out, was it?'

Emma looked at him in despair. He would never believe that her father had not been to blame for that dreadful accident, and it grieved her that she had never been able to prove his innocence.

'I wish that I could go back and change what happened,' she said, swallowing hard, 'but I can't do that. Above all, I'm sorry that your sister was hurt.'

'We're all sorry,' he said, his mouth making a bitter twist, 'but there doesn't seem to be much that we can do about it.'

Emma's heart sank. Things would never be resolved between them, would they? He blamed her father for his sister's pain, and she could do nothing to put things right.

Her father was a good man, a decent citizen who would never willingly harm others, and she knew in her heart that he had not been responsible for what had gone on that day. He always followed the rule book, and it was inconceivable that he had been negligent in any way.

Why was it that she and her mother were the only ones who believed that? Would she ever be able to get Rhys and his family to see things from her point of view?

CHAPTER TWO

THE reporter hadn't wasted any time at all, had he? Emma stared down at the newspaper, exasperation flooding through her. Up to now she had been enjoying the early morning sunshine, eating her breakfast toast at a table out in the paved courtyard at the back of her London flat, but now she put down the half-eaten slice.

There it was, all laid out before her, the whole sorry tale of the boating accident, accompanied by photos of the ambulance at the scene, with the wrecked boats in the background. Along with that, there was another picture, one of the helicopter, showing Emma standing in front of it, looking straight into the camera lens.

She sat back in her garden seat and scanned the article, her mouth tightening as she digested its contents. Why couldn't he have left things alone? Not content with relating the details of the incident, the journalist had taken it on himself to dredge up a collection of facts about Emma, including a brief mention of the explosion that had taken place at her father's restaurant some two years ago.

A noise disturbed her and dragged her attention from the paper to the house that adjoined hers.

'Don't let Samson jump up at you like that, Kayla. He's filthy.' Emma's neighbour came in off the footpath and pushed open the gate of the garden next door. 'I just can't believe how this dog manages to get himself in such a mess every time we go out. I swear he attracts dirt like a magnet.' Lindsey took hold of the dog's lead and marched the spaniel towards the house, stopping only to wave at Emma over the trellised fence that separated the two properties. 'Any chance of a cup of coffee?' she called out.

Emma nodded. 'It'll have to be a fairly quick one, though, because I have to go to work in a few minutes. Come round. It's already percolating.'

Four-year-old Kayla beat her mother to it, coming through the side gate to join Emma on the small paved terrace. 'Samson went in the brook again,' she said, shaking her head and making her blonde curls shimmer, 'and Mummy's very cross. She hasn't got time to bath him, 'cos she has to go to work.'

'Me, too. We're all in a bit of a rush. I expect Samson will have to go in the bath later on.' Emma smiled at the little girl. 'Do you want some juice?'

'Yes, please.' Kayla looked at the newspaper that was lying on the table and turned to Emma with an awed expression in her bright blue eyes. 'Is that a picture of you?'

Emma nodded. 'That's right, it is.'

The child turned as her mother came to join them a

minute or so later. 'Look, Mummy…it's Emma in the paper.'

'I know…I saw it before we went out.' Lindsey sat down and accepted the coffee that Emma pushed towards her, while Kayla went to examine the pots of flowering plants that decorated one corner of the yard. 'Thanks,' Lindsey said. 'I'm well and truly ready for this.'

She was an attractive young woman, with blonde hair that was cut into a shining bob and pinned back from her heart-shaped face with gold clips. Now, though, she was frowning as she looked down at the newspaper. 'I didn't realise that you had been caught up in an explosion,' she said. 'It must have been awful.'

'It was. I was helping out in the restaurant at the time, during one of my weekends off. There was a lot of fallen masonry, but we managed to keep the fire back, with the help of people from the neighbouring businesses, at least until the firemen came and took over.'

'The article mentioned a woman who was injured.'

'Yes, she was a friend of mine…my boss's sister, actually. Most people escaped with minor injuries, thankfully, but she was trapped under some rubble and the firemen had to pull her out. It turned out that she had a broken pelvis.'

Lindsey winced. 'That sounds nasty.'

Emma nodded. 'It makes me shudder even now to think about it. I can't imagine how we would have felt if anyone had been killed.'

'The person who wrote the article didn't seem too

sympathetic,' Lindsey commented, sipping her coffee. 'He put a bit of a slant on things, I thought. It was only a sentence or two, but it was all very negative. Do you know him?'

'Yes… I'd seen him around before any of this happened, when he was busy covering various local issues, and then, of course, he came to interview people at the restaurant. When it was all over, he tried to chat me up and ask me out on a date, but I turned him down… I tried to be diplomatic about it, but can you imagine how I was feeling? My friend had just been badly injured and my father's business was in ruins.'

Lindsey winced. 'A case of really bad timing, I'd say.'

'You're right. I think that's probably the reason why he's a touch hostile towards me now.' She sighed. 'Still, it can't be helped. There's nothing much I can do about it. It's just unfortunate that he's decided to rake over everything again. It could start people gossiping, and dredge up old animosities.'

They talked for a while longer, and then Emma finished off her toast and brushed crumbs from her fingers. 'I shall have to go,' she said with a wry smile. 'I doubt they'll keep the helicopter waiting for me if I'm not there.'

'Me, too. I have to take Kayla to nursery school.' Lindsey got to her feet. 'I'll see you later, Emma.'

Emma watched them go, and then hurried to get the tube into work. She didn't know whether she was glad to be seeing Rhys again or apprehensive. Where he was concerned, her emotions were in a state of constant turmoil, and it seemed to Emma that they had always been this way, ever since she had first come to know him.

He didn't appear to have any such qualms. When she walked into their headquarters, he looked at her in an odd fashion, studying her through narrowed eyes, almost as though he hadn't expected her to turn up for work that morning.

'Is something wrong?' she asked. She sent a wary glance over the skirt and cotton top that she was wearing, and then checked the mass of her burnished curls with a hand to make sure that nothing was out of place. 'I'm not late, am I? I went to check up on the patients we brought in yesterday.'

'No, you're bang on time.' He frowned. 'Checking up isn't part of the job, you know.'

She nodded. 'I know, but I wanted to find out for myself how they were doing. It looks as though they've all come through just fine…the man with the head injury is awake and responsive now, but you knew that, didn't you? The staff nurse told me that you'd asked to be kept informed.' He was just as dedicated to their patients' welfare as everyone else, if the truth were known. He just didn't want to own up to it.

He gave a brief smile. 'You've got me there. I like to know whether or not we've had some success. It makes the job worthwhile when we manage to pull people through.'

She went and changed into her uniform, and then

came to join the team around the table. As she approached, Rhys moved to gather up his medical bag, pushing a newspaper to one side at the same time. Emma glanced at it, and there was a sinking feeling in her stomach when she realised that it was the same paper she and Lindsey had read.

She grimaced. It looked as though soon everyone would be reminded of what had happened two years ago and how her father was a figure of hate.

There was no time to dwell on any of that, though, because Rhys's grey gaze meshed with hers, and he said abruptly, 'We're on the move. We've just had a callout to an area near Swanley, south of the Thames. There's been a riding accident. A woman has had a fall from a horse, and the paramedics say it's a spinal injury.'

'Will we take her to the nearest unit that specialises in spinal injuries?'

'Yes, that's what they're asking us to do.'

They were already heading towards the helicopter as they were speaking, and Emma could only hope that the woman was not as badly hurt as everyone feared. If the spinal cord was badly damaged, it could mean that she would be sentenced to a life confined in a wheelchair.

James took them up and away, flying over the city and heading southeast towards the Kent countryside. Soon they had left behind them the built-up area surrounding the Thames and the landscape beneath them turned to green fields and low-lying hills, dotted with scattered farmsteads and pockets of dense woodland. It was beautiful to look at, but Emma was tense, wondering what lay ahead.

As soon as they had landed on a flattened area of ground bordering a meadow, the team jumped down from the helicopter and were met by a police officer.

'She's through here,' he said, leading the way, and they hurried along a well-worn bridleway towards a small copse.

The woman was lying on the ground, unmoving, and Emma could see that the attending paramedic had already placed a collar around her neck to secure her cervical spine, while his colleague was giving her oxygen. He came over to them.

'I'm Simon,' he said. 'The patient is Melanie Thomas, and she's twenty-six years old. She can't feel her legs, but there's movement and feeling in her upper limbs.'

Rhys went to examine the woman.

'Was she thrown from the horse?' Emma asked. 'Do we know anything about how this came about?'

'Only that she was unseated as she tried to jump a fence. We think the horse must have been startled by something and he reared up, causing her to be jerked backwards. She landed on her back and smacked into that fallen tree branch.' He indicated a bough that had been removed from beneath the woman and tossed to one side. 'We're still trying to locate her husband so that we can tell him what's happened.'

None of it sounded good, and Emma could see that Rhys was beginning to look concerned. He murmured softly, 'Her pulse is thready. I think there's been some bleeding into her lower back, so I'm going to give her corticosteroids to try to reduce the swelling.'

Emma knelt down beside the woman and set about putting up two intravenous lines for saline and crystalloid solutions, so that they could allay any onset of shock and replace vital fluids.

'I want to get her moved onto the stretcher,' Rhys said, after a while, 'but we need to take care that her whole spine stays in the neutral position. We'll do a four person lift, on my count.'

Emma nodded, and they worked together, with Martin and Simon lining up alongside Melanie and helping to carefully move her onto the stretcher. 'Let's get some sandbags on either side of her head and secure them with tape,' Rhys said, when they had finished.

'How are you doing?' he asked the young woman a short time later, looking at her with compassion and checking for any immediate signs of discomfort.

'I'm all right,' Melanie said, her voice breaking. She fought for control. 'What will happen to my baby? Will it be all right?'

'Your baby?' Rhys's eyes widened a fraction, and though he tried not to show that he was disturbed by this new piece of information, Emma knew him well enough to know that he was worried. He glanced at Simon, but the paramedic shook his head, showing that this was news to him, too.

'How far along is the pregnancy?' Rhys asked.

'Twenty weeks.' Melanie's voice was strained. 'I really want this baby. Please, don't let anything happen to it.'

Rhys pulled in a quick breath, but then stopped to

reassure her. 'We're doing everything that we can to make sure that you're safe,' he said.

'No, you don't understand...' Melanie's face crumpled. 'I'm not worried for myself. I can't lose this baby...I can't.'

'I know,' Rhys said quietly, 'but you must try to stay calm. We need to get you to hospital now, but once we're in the helicopter, I'll examine you again to make sure that you're doing OK.'

He supervised her transfer to the helicopter, and then turned to Emma. 'We had better check for any bleeding,' he said in a low voice, 'and we should take some blood for cross-matching. I'll ask the copilot to call ahead so that they have an obstetrician standing by.'

Once they were airborne, they examined Melanie once more, and Emma said, 'There's some bleeding and the foetal heartbeat is fluctuating. If there's any chance that the placenta could have been torn away from the uterine wall, even partially, perhaps we should tilt the stretcher so that Melanie's feet are higher than her head.'

'Yes, let's do it...and we'll keep a careful eye on her pulse oximeter readings as well. We need to be sure that the foetus is getting enough oxygen.'

They touched down on the hospital's helipad a few minutes later, and Emma hurried alongside the trolley as Rhys and Martin wheeled their patient to the lift. There they handed her over to the waiting medical team, reporting swiftly on her condition.

'Thanks, we'll take it from here,' the neurologist

said, and Emma felt a sense of letdown, a feeling of a job only half-done. She didn't want to leave Melanie.

Their work here was finished and so they walked back to the helicopter and started to head back to base. Rhys was silent on the journey, his features tense, and she guessed that he was battling with more than straightforward concern for his patient.

From the straight set of his mouth, she had the idea that he was thinking back to how his sister's fate had been similar to Melanie's. Two years ago Amy had suffered more than a broken pelvis. She had also lost her baby, and the tragedy had affected the whole family.

'What are her chances, do you think?' Martin asked, cutting into her thoughts as they arrived back on firm ground and started to walk towards their headquarters.

'It's too early to say,' she answered. 'It depends what the ultrasound scan shows and to what degree the placenta has been dislodged. If there's only a small amount of bleeding, things may settle in time. As for the spinal injury, she'll need an MRI scan to show what damage has been done. Things look pretty bleak at the moment, but there might just be a chance that it's not as bad as it seems.'

She went over to the filter machine that was housed to one side of the room, and helped herself to coffee. Rhys was already there, his expression bleak as he nursed a mug in his hand and took a long swallow of the hot liquid.

'Are you thinking about Amy?' Emma asked. It took all her courage to bring up the subject, and she half expected to be rebuffed for her trouble, but she had to know. There had to be some way she could break through the barrier of silence that had sprung up between them. 'Seeing Melanie in that state must have brought things back to you.'

He nodded. 'It was hard, seeing her go through that, hearing her plead with me to save her child. Amy said the same thing to me at the time of the explosion. She begged me to help her. "I can't lose this baby," she said. I can still hear those words in my mind now.'

'Surely you can't blame yourself? You did everything you could for your sister—no one could have done anything more. She was hurt too badly.' Emma's gaze was stricken as she watched him. Her voice faded. 'We all know how desperately she wanted that baby. She and Elliot had been through so much, for so long, in order to be able to conceive, and it was a terrible blow when she lost it.'

She tried to keep her voice on an even keel. 'I keep asking myself why she was the one who had to suffer, but there's never any answer to that question, is there? I wish I could make it up to Amy in some way, but I can't, and that leaves me feeling helpless. We can't turn back the clock and make things work out differently.'

'I don't blame myself.' Rhys's voice was terse. 'You're not at fault either. We all did what we could for her, but the fact is the explosion should never have happened in the first place. My sister's marriage is on the rocks simply because your father didn't take adequate precautions to keep his restaurant safe for everyone who used it.' He looked at her, his gaze steady.

'That's what none of us is able to come to terms with. That's what my family can't forgive.'

'Her marriage is failing?' Emma's brow furrowed. 'I didn't know it had come to that. I thought Elliot would support her through all this—he was just as upset as she was.'

Rhys's jaw was clenched. 'I'm just telling you how it is. Losing the baby was the last straw. Amy can't reconcile herself to it, and Elliot couldn't cope when she sank into a deep depression. He didn't know what to do, or how to react, and in the end she seemed to distance herself from him and withdrew into a shell. He couldn't reach her.'

Emma moistened her dry lips with the tip of her tongue. 'I didn't realise that. I'm sorry it has turned out that way. I wanted to help her through all this, and I tried to talk to her on a number of occasions, but she snubbed me and I thought it was just me that she had turned against. We were such friends, and then...then there was nothing. Our friendship seemed to fizzle out and there was nothing I could do to prevent it happening. I didn't realise it had affected all other areas of her life.'

Rhys put down his coffee-cup and straightened up. 'We've all had to cope with the aftermath. My parents have always been optimists, and they tried to encourage Amy to look to the future and hope for some silver lining, but no good has ever come out of this situation. Just this last month Amy and Elliot have decided to go their separate ways. Elliot is looking around for a place of his own.'

Emma absorbed that and was silent for a while, thinking things through. Rhys was bitter, and she could see why he would feel that way. He had a strong bond with his sister.

For her part, Emma had grieved for a long time because the explosion had wrought tragedy in so many ways and had touched so many lives. Those who had been less severely injured would bear the psychological scars for years to come.

Even so, there was a bit of her that rebelled against her father being continually made the scapegoat. She knew him better than anyone, except for her mother, and instinctively she was convinced that he hadn't been responsible for what had happened that day.

'My father did what he could to help your sister. He was devastated by what happened to her, and he stayed with her throughout, waiting until the emergency services arrived and trying to keep her safe. Then he helped to lift the beam that had fallen on her. Do you think he could go through all that and not be affected by what happened?'

'I'm sure he was, but that doesn't change anything, does it?'

Frustration washed over her. 'You think he hasn't suffered, too? He lost everything that he had built up and worked for over the years. It was his dream to own a restaurant, to follow on with what his father had started before him. It was destroyed that day and his world fell apart. The insurance company wouldn't pay out because everyone accused him of negligence, of not following health and safety rules. He had to start all over again.'

Rhys gave a wry grimace. 'I heard that he was doing all right for himself, and you said yourself that he has managed to buy another property—I even heard rumours that he wants to start up another restaurant on the ground floor of the place he's doing up.'

'That's true, but he's had to pay a heavy price for all that. My parents had to lose the house that they loved. Now he's mortgaged to the hilt, and at his time of life that isn't a good place to be. It was a question of sink or swim, and he chose to take a deep breath and do his utmost to rise above the tide. I admire him for that. Things have gone badly for him, and it shouldn't have turned out that way, because he didn't do what he was accused of...he wasn't responsible for what happened.'

Rhys's brow rose. 'Then who was responsible?'

Emma subsided in defeat. 'I don't know.' She stared up at him. 'Someone must have put the gas cylinder in place. Perhaps one of the workers got it out and dislodged the safety valve—but no one would admit to it. My father tried to make sure that he employed people who were trustworthy and who could be relied on, but there was always bound to be a steady turnover of staff in that kind of business.'

She frowned, thinking things through. 'He had the gas cylinders stored away under lock and key, and he thought he had done everything to safeguard the place, but a number of people knew where the keys were kept. When the restaurant was busy, any one of them could have gone and replaced the gas cylinder if it was needed.'

She hesitated. 'In fact, the kitchen doors were open that day because of the heat and there was a lot of coming and going to the barbecue out on the terrace. As I recall, we were rushed off our feet. It wouldn't have taken much for anyone to have come in from outside to take a look around, and I doubt the key cupboard was too difficult to find.'

She looked at Rhys but his expression was sceptical. 'Wasn't all that looked into at the time? I didn't hear of anything coming of that.'

Emma winced. She wasn't going to make any headway with Rhys, was she? He simply wasn't open to persuasion, and that distressed her, but there was no point in banging her head against a wall any longer.

'I hope Melanie's problems have a better outcome,' she said softly, starting to turn away from him.

'Whether or not she loses the baby is probably the least of Melanie's troubles. She has to wait and see if she'll even be able to walk after this.'

That was certainly true, and it wasn't something that Emma wanted to contemplate. She had taken up a career in medicine because she had hoped above all to save lives, but the downside of her work was altogether too heartrending.

She went over to the table, where James, the pilot, was studying a maintenance procedures checklist. He looked up as she approached, and ran a hand through his dark hair.

'Is there something wrong between you and Rhys?' he ventured in a low tone. He studied her, his hazel eyes gently probing.

Emma frowned. 'Why do you ask that?' She glanced over to the corner of the room where the coffee-machine was housed, but Rhys was no longer standing there. It appeared that he had gone outside to take a breath of air.

'It's just that there seems to be some tension between the two of you. I noticed it yesterday when you first met up in here, and it was there again just now. How well do you know one another? Is it going to be a problem for you to work together?'

'There are just some matters that we disagree on. I'm sure we're both professional enough that we'll be able to ignore our differences and concentrate on the job in hand.' Her green eyes were troubled. Things were pretty bad if a colleague had noticed that there was friction between them.

She said carefully, 'We used to live in the same village, so I suppose it was inevitable that my sister and I would come to know Rhys and his sister. We often went around together, on country walks and to village functions, though, of course, they were from a different world to us, both financially and socially. His family was very prominent in the village, and his parents were into all kinds of fundraising and community issues.'

'So you've known each other for a long time?'

She nodded. 'We haven't seen much of each other in the last few years, though. He left to go and do his medical training, and then, once he had qualified, he went on to specialise. I was a few years behind him when I started my own medical career, so we tended to only meet up when either of us went home for the weekend or for longer breaks.'

She had missed him dreadfully when he had gone away, but she wasn't about to tell James that.

Rhys had meant the world to her. Throughout the years she had known him, he had always been affectionate and teasing towards her, and she had begun to cherish the times when she had been alone with him.

Despite this, she had known for a long time that Rhys wanted to work in A and E, and it had come as no surprise when he had eventually left home. Her heart had gone with him, but all the same she had wished him well.

He was quick thinking and intelligent, full of energy and determination, and she had known that he would succeed wherever his ambitions led him.

Her one consolation had been that she believed she would be able to see him from time to time. She winced. Who could have foreseen that things would take a downward turn? After the accident their friendship seemed to have fallen by the wayside, and that grieved her. Everything had changed and she didn't know how to bring things back to how they had been before.

Would she and Rhys ever again experience the rapport that they had once shared?

CHAPTER THREE

SAMSON'S ears were pricked up, on the alert, and he was barking again, the pitch getting louder and more insistent by the minute.

'Something's definitely rattling him,' Lindsey said, casting a troubled glance over her dog. 'This is the third night in a row that he's been spooked. I wish I knew what was causing him to behave like this.' She frowned. 'You know, earlier today I thought I saw someone hanging about near the hedge.'

'Did you?' Emma frowned, twitching back the living-room curtain and peering out into the darkness. As her eyes became accustomed to the gloom, she could gradually make out the shapes of the trees and shrubs in her small front garden.

She couldn't see anything untoward. Beyond the garden, the street was empty and there was no movement as far as she could tell. 'Everything seems quiet enough, and there's no sign of anything or anyone out there now.'

Lindsey came to join Emma at the window. 'It's

strange, though, isn't it? I wonder what's causing him to act like this? Maybe it's that journalist. Could it be that he's following you in the hope of getting another angle on the story? Or maybe he's not given up on that date he wanted.'

'Heaven forbid.' Emma let the curtain fall back into place and walked over to the spaniel, stroking his silky smooth head. 'What's troubling you, lad? Are you hearing things?'

'Perhaps he needs his ears cleaning out,' Lindsey said with a laugh, and Emma smiled.

'You're probably right at that.' She picked up the bottle of wine from the table and inspected its contents. 'There's a glass or two left in here. Do you want some more?'

Lindsey shook her head and looked over to where Kayla was sitting, playing with her doll on the soft rug. 'No, thanks. I really should be getting back to my own place. It's past Kayla's bedtime.' She sighed. 'Perhaps when Tom gets back from Switzerland in a week or so, we'll be able to have a proper girls' night together.'

'Sounds good to me.' Emma started to clear away the wineglasses, placing them on the kitchen drainer at the far side of the room. Her flat was compact, made up of a bedroom, a bathroom and a living room with an open-plan kitchen. It wasn't huge, but it was neat and clean, and the windows were placed to let in lots of light during the daytime.

She saw Lindsey and Kayla out a few minutes later. French doors led out from the living room into the tiny courtyard, and all they had to do was walk from there to their own garden and in through the back door of their own flat. Emma watched them go, and when she saw that they were safely inside, she went back into her living room and locked the doors. Samson was quiet as he followed them, but Emma wasn't taking any chances.

At work next day, Emma felt as though she was hungover. She muddled through the morning, conscious that she had to give her best, and worried because she was finding that so difficult to do. The fact that her brain was foggy had nothing to do with the wine that she had drunk, but far more to do with lack of sleep. She was still concerned about why Samson was unnerved. It worried her that someone might be hanging around the place, and she was left feeling insecure, on edge.

'Have you been there?'

The drone of the helicopter almost wiped out the words. Shaken out of her trance, Emma looked up at Rhys. He was watching her, a questioning look in his eyes. 'I'm sorry,' she said. 'Did you say something? I was miles away.'

'So I gathered.' His mouth made a wry twist. 'I was just pointing out Richmond Park below us, and I was asking you if you'd ever been to Pembroke Lodge, maybe had lunch there at some time?'

She frowned, pausing to look at the landscape laid out beneath them. They were passing over a stretch of water and she could see deer grazing on the grassland below.

Ahead of them, a magnificent white porticoed

building, a Georgian mansion, nestled in beautifully landscaped grounds. 'Is that it?' she asked.

He nodded, and she said, 'No. I've always meant to go there and try it out, but I've never quite managed it. Is it worth a visit?'

'I think you would like it. It was built on high ground, and the views from there are fantastic. On a clear day you can see across the Thames valley and beyond, as far as Windsor.'

They had been heading west, and as they passed over the golf course and the botanic gardens she saw the river ahead of them. The pilot began to sweep the aircraft in a northward arc.

'We'll be at our destination any minute now,' Rhys said.

They flew onwards, following the course of a canal, passing over a series of locks. People were walking along the towpath, enjoying the summer's day, and Emma half wished that she could join them. Then they left the countryside behind, and a network of roads started to take its place.

Inside the helicopter, they started to prepare for action. They had been called out to a road traffic accident, and Emma was slightly apprehensive as to what they would find. A lorry had overturned, coming off the motorway, and a motorcyclist had had the misfortune to be caught up in the chaos.

'Let's go,' Rhys said, as they touched down. He and Martin moved swiftly, sprinting ahead of her, and Emma did her best to keep up with them.

The lorry driver was in a bad way. He was conscious, but his skin had an unhealthy pallor, and he was confused, finding it painful and difficult to breathe. His neck veins were engorged, and his heart rate was way too fast. His blood pressure was falling.

Firemen were doing their best to release him from the cab, but they stopped for long enough to allow Emma to climb in beside him and attend to his injuries. Rhys went with Martin to examine the motorcyclist.

'Jack, I think you have broken several ribs,' she said to the driver, after she had made a swift examination. 'It looks as though they have penetrated your lungs and the pleura, and that's why you're having difficulty in breathing. Air has entered the pleural cavity, but it can't escape, and so pressure has built up, causing your lung to collapse. I need to try to re-inflate the lung.'

'Do what you have to, Doctor,' Jack said in a rasping voice.

She nodded, already preparing a syringe. 'I'll give you a painkiller first.' As soon as she had done that, she identified the second intercostal space in the midclavicular line, and then inserted the cannula just above the third rib. There was a satisfying hiss of air escaping. Quickly, she removed the internal metal needle and taped the plastic cannula in place.

'Is your breathing a little easier now?' she asked.

He nodded, but he was growing weaker by the minute, and he closed his eyes.

Emma was already preparing an intravenous line in order to give him vital fluids. When she had examined him, there was some abdominal tenderness in the right upper quadrant, and she was afraid that he might also have sustained liver and spleen injuries. She needed to get him to hospital and to Theatre where a surgeon could operate to repair any damage. In the meantime, he could be bleeding internally.

'Are you hurting anywhere else?' she asked.

He indicated his left shoulder, and that helped to confirm her diagnosis. A build-up of blood from an injured spleen might cause referred pain like that.

Rhys came to join her. 'How are you doing?' he asked, sending her a swift glance. 'We need to get these people to hospital now. My patient has abdominal trauma. I suspect he has a split pancreas, and we need to get him to surgery fast. There's nothing I can do to control the bleeding.'

Did he think that she was working too slowly? 'Same here,' she said under her breath. She was going as quickly as she could. 'I need to put in a chest drain— give me a couple more minutes, will you?'

'I'll give you a hand.'

It was difficult for the two of them to work in such cramped conditions. The firemen were doing their best to continue with their rescue operation while Emma and Rhys worked, but Emma knew that she had to go on. Blood was building up inside her patient's chest cavity, causing more pressure, and though he was breathing oxygen through a mask, he was still in a critical condition.

This time she identified the fifth intercostal space,

anterior to the mid-axillary line. She cleaned the area and infiltrated a local anaesthetic into the skin and pleura. Then she made a transverse incision parallel to the line of the ribs, pierced the pleura, using the blunt end of the clamp, and inserted the chest drain, clamping the opposite end. Finally, she attached the end to an underwater seal and released the clamp, ensuring the free flow of blood.

Rhys sutured the tube in position and taped it in place.

Emma frowned as she watched gas bubble through the underwater drain. 'That doesn't look good,' she said in a low voice, turning away so that Jack wouldn't hear.

'No, it doesn't,' Rhys agreed. 'We'd better have a cardiothoracic surgeon standing by.'

Emma pulled in a deep breath, but Rhys was already on the move, calling for the firemen to release the patient. 'We need to get him on a stretcher and into the helicopter, as fast as you can.'

A few minutes later, their patients were on board, and the pilot turned the helicopter back towards the hospital. Rhys's patient was in a bad way. He had a nasogastric tube in place, along with two intravenous lines, and he was being given oxygen. As soon as they reached the hospital, he would need a CT scan to determine the extent of the damage.

A team was waiting to meet them the instant they landed. Handing over, Emma once again felt the lack of closure, the need to stay with her patients and follow through to the end.

Perhaps Rhys read her thoughts. 'You have already made a difference to the outcome,' he said. 'You gave them lifesaving treatment, and now it's down to others to carry on. The job we do relies on teamwork, on everyone playing a part.' He looked at her. 'You shouldn't feel bad about letting go. You did well.'

'Perhaps... I can't quite get used to handing over. You've been doing it for a lot longer than I have, and perhaps it's easier for you.'

Martin and the others had already gone back to base, but Emma was restless, and for the moment she couldn't face going back to the unit.

'Do you want to grab a bite to eat?' Rhys asked. 'I have some lunch in my pack, and we could share it out here in the fresh air—over by the wall, if you like. There's some shade there, and less of a breeze.'

She stared up at him. 'I didn't have time to make sandwiches this morning. Are you sure you have enough for both of us?'

He nodded. 'I always bring extra, just in case.' He led her towards a sheltered corner of the roof terrace, and they sat down on a bench. He removed a canvas bag from his pack and spread out the contents on a low wooden table. There was chicken and scotch eggs, a container with sandwiches and a small bowl of ready-made salad. He had even brought along bottled water.

'Help yourself.'

'Thanks.' She picked out a chicken drumstick and nibbled at salad, then wiped her hands on a serviette. 'This is good. I was more hungry than I realised.'

He studied her thoughtfully. 'I think perhaps you needed time to wind down. You've been out of sorts all day, haven't you?'

'Was it that noticeable?'

'It was. Is it anything you want to talk about?'

She shook her head. 'Not really. I'm not at all sure what it is that's bothering me. There's nothing that I can put my finger on.'

He looked at her through narrowed eyes, and she found herself noticing inconsequentially that his lashes were thick and dark, and his grey eyes were all-seeing, as though nothing could escape him.

'Are you still worried about the article in the paper the other day?'

'What makes you think that I was worried?'

Rhys shrugged. 'I've known you for a long time, remember. You're very defensive about your father…and besides that, there were some personal details that could have seemed invasive.' He was still watching her, in that steady way of his, and she swallowed, trying not to let his scrutiny disturb her. 'Has the reporter been back to bother you? I had the feeling that he wanted to do another article…to delve into what your father is working on now.'

'He won't get very far if he tries. Not if I have anything to do with it, anyhow. He can snoop as much as he likes, but he won't get anywhere very fast.'

'So he has been bothering you?'

She grimaced. 'I wouldn't say that, exactly. Someone has been hanging around, I think. I'm not quite sure what to make of it. Perhaps I'm imagining things.' She braced herself. 'I'm probably overtired, a little out of sorts, that's all. It's nothing to worry about.'

He moved along the seat, sliding closer to her. 'If it's going to affect you at work, then it's something that we should both be concerned about, don't you think?' He put an arm around her shoulders. 'If there's anything at all, you should tell me about it.'

It was a long time since she'd been this close to him. It was just a casual gesture on his part, born of familiarity from all those times they had hung around together as teenagers and beyond, but to Emma it was something far more. His touch heated her skin, turned her blood to flame. It was impossible to ignore the gentle caress. His fingers cupped her shoulder, urged her towards him, to face him, and his head tilted to one side, as though by some magnetic impulse he would draw her to look into his eyes.

She tried to resist, fighting the urge that compelled her, but his gaze tangled with hers and he studied her face, reading the confusion in her green eyes.

'Do you think he's watching the house?'

'I think he might be.'

He was thoughtful for a moment or two. 'I could come over and check the place out for you, if you like. If nothing else, he might see me and realise that you're not alone. It might be enough to put him off. He's not to know that I don't live there.'

'I don't know.' She tugged lightly at her lower lip with her teeth. 'It's probably nothing, and I don't want to put you to any trouble.'

'You aren't.' He squeezed her gently, drawing her closer to him, so close that she could feel the beat of his heart and absorb the warmth that came from him.

She wanted to lean her head against his shoulder and give herself up to this tender moment. It felt good, having him hold her this way, but at the back of her mind a warning bell was beginning to make itself heard. It wouldn't do for her to accept his help and allow herself to care for him, would it? His opinion of her father wouldn't change, and his family would always be antagonistic towards her. Knowing what had happened to their daughter, they wouldn't find it easy to forgive, and they would certainly never forget. Most of all, would they ever come to believe that her father hadn't been to blame?

Emma eased herself away from Rhys. One day, she would prove her father's innocence. She would put an end to all the gossip and speculation, once and for all. Quite how she was going to achieve this, she wasn't sure, but in the meantime she would stay loyal to him and defend him from anyone who pointed a finger of accusation...even Rhys.

'Are you OK?' Rhys was looking at her doubtfully.

'Yes, I'm fine.'

'Are you sure? This can be a difficult job at the best of times. You can't afford to be carrying around a mess of troubles. They cloud your judgement and slow you down when you need to be clear-thinking and level-headed.'

'I'm sure.' She felt deflated all at once. That was what this was all about, wasn't it? He was making sure that his team was on the ball, that everyone measured up. It wasn't personal. It had never been personal.

She took a drink of the water he offered her, and then said on a light note, 'I expect we should go and join the others. Judging by the number of calls we've already had today, we've not finished by a long way.'

He accepted her mood change without comment, and after a minute or two they cleared away the impromptu picnic and went back to headquarters.

Some three hours later, when her shift ended, Emma went to see how their patients were doing. More than anything, she was worried about Melanie, who had been thrown from her horse a few days ago. Surely there would be some news by now?

'I rang the spinal injuries unit to check up for you. It isn't as bad as we first thought,' the staff nurse told her when she called in on her. 'It's beginning to look as though her spinal cord is intact. There was a compressive lesion, but she had surgery to alleviate that, and we think she'll be back on her feet eventually, once the swelling has settled down.'

'That's a relief.' Emma ventured a smile. 'What about the baby, though? Is there any good news there?'

Staff nurse nodded. 'Things seem to be healing up there, too. There was just a small tear, and it seems to have righted itself. She'll need to rest, of course, but the baby doesn't appear to have been harmed in any way.'

'I'm so pleased about that.' She said goodbye to the nurse and headed towards the exit doors. 'I'll keep in touch,' she said.

'I hope you will. It's good for the patients, too. They often want to thank the doctors who brought them in.'

Emma set off for home. She was tired after her day's work, and she was more than a little distracted after the way Rhys had held her in his arms. She wanted to forget that it had ever happened, but the memory remained imprinted on her mind, and refused to go away.

She would be glad to put her feet up and lose herself in a good book, but the day wasn't done with her yet. Another surprise awaited her when she arrived home.

'I wondered if I would bump into you,' a man said, as she was about to put the key in her front door. 'I just moved into a place across the road, and I thought I remembered that you lived around here.'

Emma recognised the voice. Turning around, she saw Rhys's brother-in-law coming towards her.

'Elliot?' Her eyes widened, and she looked at him closely as he came to stand beside her. He hadn't changed at all since she had last seen him. His hair was black, with a slight wave at the front. His eyes were dark, too, a sombre grey that seemed to reflect his mood right now.

She pulled herself together. 'Did I hear you say that you have come to live around here?'

'That's right.' His mouth made a grimace that might have been intended as a smile. 'I suppose you must have heard that Amy and I have separated?'

'Yes, I did.' She frowned. 'I'm sorry. I always thought you were so happy together.'

'We were, mostly...until we lost the baby. Then everything started to go downhill.'

Emma stiffened. She realised that she was waiting for the recriminations to start up, but Elliot didn't say any more, and after a moment she said hesitantly, 'Is there a chance that you'll get back together again, do you think?'

He looked uncomfortable. 'I don't know. All I know is that it became impossible for us to live together any longer. She told me she thought it would be better if I left, so after a while I started to look around for a place of my own.'

'I'm sorry.' She didn't know what to say to him. 'Sorry' seemed such an inadequate word. 'I suppose it must have been quite difficult for you to find somewhere suitable.'

He nodded. 'Given that now I'm having to pay for two properties, yes, it was, but I imagine things will sort themselves out in time.'

He was a solicitor, hardworking and intelligent, and he had deserved every bit of his success, but he was young and he was still establishing himself in his field. She wouldn't have imagined that he would come to live anywhere near here, but perhaps it wasn't so unusual. There were quick links from here to the City, and most of the people who lived in the area were young professionals. The properties were modernised and reasonably priced, and if he was still maintaining the family home, she guessed this would suit his pocket.

'Are you settling in all right?'

'More or less. It takes some getting used to.'

She made a faint smile. 'I imagine it would.' She was

thoughtful for a moment, and then said, 'Do you want to come in for a coffee? I've only just finished work, and I was planning on heating up a casserole for supper. You could join me, if you like.'

'If you're sure it's no trouble.'

'I'm sure. Come on in.'

They were finishing off the meal some half an hour later when the doorbell rang. 'It's probably Lindsey, my neighbour,' Emma said, going to answer it. 'She often pops round in the evening, especially when her husband is away.'

It wasn't Lindsey. Rhys was standing by the porch, looking at her with the quizzical expression she had come to know so well, and Emma's mouth opened and closed in a kind of shock.

'I wasn't expecting you,' she said.

'Weren't you? I thought we said that I would come around, if only to warn off your stalker.' He waited. 'Aren't you going to invite me in?'

'I…uh, yes, of course.' She took a step back and opened the door wider. 'I don't actually have a stalker. I think I was just imagining things. I haven't seen anyone near the place this evening.'

'That's good. Perhaps if he sees my car parked outside, he'll stay away.'

He followed her along the corridor towards the living room, stopping to admire the artwork that adorned the walls at intervals along the way.

'I recognise that one,' he said, indicating a country scene, a gentle wash of greens and gold and hazy blue sky, the bark of a tree picked out in oils, the leaves a medley of dappled sunlight and shades of autumn. 'I've seen it before somewhere. Isn't it your sister's work?'

'That's right. She gave it to me when I moved in here.'

'I think I recognise the place.' He studied the picture more closely. 'Isn't that the dip near the brook by Bluebell Copse…the place where we all used to go blackberry picking in the summer?'

'It is.' Emma held her breath. He couldn't know just how much that small part of their home village meant to her, could he?

That was where she had first realised that she was falling in love with Rhys. He had stood tall and strong, smiling into her eyes as he'd held back the brambles so that she could walk through to the meadow beyond. It had been a teasing smile and it had melted her heart, but she had never been able to bring herself to tell him how she felt about him.

He looked at the painting for a moment longer, taking it in, before he turned away and continued down the hallway. 'It's all very clean and bright in here,' he murmured. 'Was it like this when you moved in, or have you added your own touches?'

'I decorated it throughout,' she answered slowly. 'It didn't take long because there isn't very much to the place, but I wanted to make it my own.'

She hesitated before showing him into her living room. 'Actually, I have another visitor,' she told him. 'He's having supper with me.'

'Oh?' Rhys looked taken aback. 'Perhaps I'm intruding.'

'No, of course you're not. Come on through.'

Elliot was sitting at the table, in the corner that housed her kitchen units and acted as a dining room. He had finished off the remnants of the casserole, eating like a man who wasn't sure where his next meal was coming from, and now he was tucking into a slice of apple pie, generously topped with creamy custard.

Rhys stood stock still in the doorway. He didn't say anything at all for a moment, just stared at Elliot.

Elliot, in turn, stared back at Rhys. Then he put down his spoon and for a while there was silence in the room.

'I've moved into a house across the road,' he said at last. 'You know how things were with Amy and me. Something had to give, sooner or later.'

Rhys nodded. 'She's not doing too well right now. I imagine she's very upset.'

'Because I've moved out?' Elliot shook his head. 'I don't think so. She didn't react at all. I might as well not have been there for the last few months. She didn't seem to care about anything.'

'That's all part of the illness, isn't it? Depression takes people in different ways.'

'I don't think so. I had the feeling that she just didn't want me around. Our marriage has been disintegrating for quite some time.'

Rhys's glance moved over the kitchen, taking in the dinner plates that had been moved to a worktop by the sink and coming to rest on the half-eaten apple pie. 'It looks as though you've managed to find someone to fill the void,' he said.

Turning to look back at Emma, he gave an odd grimace. 'I won't take up any more of your time,' he murmured. 'I can see that you won't be needing my help in keeping unwanted visitors away.'

Emma tried to make things right. 'There's really no need for you to rush off, is there? Won't you at least stay for a while? Have a cup of coffee?'

'I don't think so.' He walked over to the door. 'I can see myself out.'

Emma hurried after him, but by the time she reached the hall he had already shut the front door behind himself.

CHAPTER FOUR

'I JUST didn't realise how bad it was at first.' The young woman was frantic, raking a hand through her brown hair, her mouth trembling as she spoke. 'Alex was playing in the field with the other children, and when his friends came to fetch me, they said he had fallen back against the stile. They told me that they had been messing about, playing fighting games, and I thought he had just bruised himself and that he would be all right.' Her voice broke. 'I couldn't understand why he wouldn't get up. I thought he was overreacting, looking for attention.'

The woman looked at Emma, her face tear-streaked. 'The paramedic said that he needed to go to a renal unit, but I don't understand—what's wrong with him? Is he going to be all right? He's only eight years old— I just can't believe this is happening.'

Emma was kneeling on the grass, making a careful examination of the little boy, while Rhys checked his blood pressure and pulse. 'We won't know the full extent of his injuries until we get him to the hospital and do some scans,' she answered quietly, 'but it looks as though he might have damaged a kidney when he fell backwards onto the stile. It may be that a rib has cracked and caused a puncture wound.' She sent the woman a quick glance. 'I'm sure you want to be with him at the hospital, so if you want to go along with the paramedic he'll see that you get a lift to the unit.'

The child's mother nodded. Pulling herself together, she leaned over to kiss her son on the cheek, and whispered, 'I'll come to you at the hospital and I'll stay with you there, Alex. Don't worry, the doctors will make sure that you're going to be all right.'

Emma hoped that she could live up to that promise. She was more than a little disturbed by the amount of livid bruising on the boy's back, in the area between the lowest rib and his pelvis, and it was becoming clear that the child's pain was getting worse.

'You've been brilliant, Alex,' she told him now. 'You've been very brave.'

The little boy was too ill to answer her, and she was very much afraid that his condition was deteriorating fast.

She glanced up at Rhys. He had finished his initial checks and was opening up his medical pack. 'I think we need to get intravenous access and start treating him for shock,' she said, taking care to keep her voice low. 'I'll give him analgesia as well, but it's worrying me that his pain level is increasing.'

Rhys began to set up an IV line. 'I agree, it's not looking good,' he said, his words pitched equally low. 'We'll have to be quick—we can't take the risk of the kidney losing its blood supply. I'll call ahead and let the team know that we'll need them to do urography. At least there'll be a nephrologist standing by.'

Emma nodded, and began to supervise the boy's transfer to the helicopter. Rhys was quiet, not saying very much, except what was essential, and she was very aware that he had had been that way all morning. He had hardly spoken a word to her, except when it was necessary, when it involved his patients. That disturbed her. It wasn't what she was used to.

But, then, perhaps she was overreacting. The day had started off badly, with a callout to a particularly nasty road traffic accident, and now they had a race against time to save this child's kidney. It should have been all in a day's work, something that she would have taken in her stride, but today her nerves were stretched to the limit and then some.

Rhys had been in a strangely withdrawn mood from the start. He hadn't said a word to her about his visit to the flat last night, but she could feel the distance between them as though he was deliberately putting up barriers.

Perhaps he was still brooding over the fact that she had invited Elliot to supper, but why should she be forced onto the defensive over that?

She had always been on good terms with Elliot. His marriage break-up wasn't anything to do with her, was it, so why should Rhys adopt a cool attitude towards her as though she had done something wrong?

As soon as Alex had been left in the capable hands of the renal team, they went back to their base. Rhys started to repack his medical bag, stocking up on items that had been used, and Emma did likewise, making a swift check of her own supplies.

'You haven't been your usual self today,' she remarked, sending him a sideways glance. 'You're very quiet.'

'Am I?'

'Yes, I think so.' She decided to tackle the issue head on. 'Is something wrong? Is it something I've done or said?'

His glance was flint sharp. 'Why on earth would you think that? As far as I'm concerned, you can say or do whatever you please.'

'But you weren't happy yesterday when you saw that Elliot was in my flat, and you left very suddenly. I was afraid that I'd offended you in some way...but I did appreciate the fact that you took the trouble to come and help me out. I want you to know that. I wasn't really expecting you to turn up, but it was very thoughtful of you to come along, all the same.'

'If I'm not saying very much, it doesn't have anything at all to do with whatever's going on in your life.' He sent her a steady look. 'I'm simply trying to work out what to do for the best for my sister. My parents are worried about her and they've asked me to help, but Amy's problems aren't something that can be resolved easily. She needs some kind of specialist counselling, but she isn't willing to get involved in any of that.'

'Oh, I see.' Emma subsided, feeling slightly foolish.

Of course he wasn't going to spend time thinking about her, or wonder about how she lived her life. She wasn't that important to him.

She said cautiously, 'Has Amy been to see a bereavement counsellor? I know the baby wasn't full term, but she suffered a loss all the same.'

'Yes, we've tried that.' His mouth made a straight line. 'There's more to it than the loss of her baby. Her marriage has fallen apart, and I suspect that she feels helpless and doesn't know how to put things right.' He sent Emma a penetrating gaze. 'Of course, it won't help matters any if she discovers that the first thing Elliot did after leaving her was to seek comfort with you.'

Emma drew herself up. 'It wasn't like that.' Her green eyes sparked. 'You make it sound as though there was something going on between us, and I resent the implication. Elliot had only just moved into his flat and he was feeling unsettled and he wanted company, someone to talk to.'

'I'm sure he did. It didn't take him long to find it, did it? Then again, he's always been very fond of you and I can't help wondering if that isn't why he chose to take up the lease on a flat in your area of all places.'

Emma stared at Rhys, tension growing in her as she realised that he wasn't going to listen to reason. How could he think that way?

She tried again. 'He just wanted to talk. He said there had been problems in the marriage for a long time. They both wanted a child, but Amy had struggled to conceive, and in the end IVF had seemed the only way for them to go. That was a problem in itself. The treatment was expensive and it was touch and go whether it would work and every failure made Amy more and more depressed.' She stared at him, her expression perplexed. 'But you must know all that.'

'I know that she needs his support now more than ever, but she isn't going to get it if he finds solace with you, is she?'

Emma clamped her lips together. He was being unfair and it wasn't at all like him. Had things deteriorated so badly between them that he couldn't see reason? His insinuations were intolerable. How could he possibly imagine that there was anything going on between Elliot and herself?

She couldn't trust herself not to say something that she would regret, and arguing with Rhys was not the way to go. Instead, she picked up her medical bag and moved away from him.

Did he really believe that she was the enemy, that she might stand between Elliot and his wife? It was incredible that he should think that way but, of course, he was worried about his sister right now, and perhaps that was making him irrational.

Emma was relieved when her shift came to an end at last. She needed time for her head to clear, for the warring thoughts that crowded in on her to be swept away. Most of all she needed space, away from Rhys.

'You're not on duty tomorrow, are you?' he asked, causing her to hesitate just as she was preparing to leave.

She shook her head. 'No… Why? Is there a problem?'

'Only that Martin won't be in either, so we'll be one member of the team short. He's going on a course in the afternoon and I'm looking for someone to fill in for him. I know it's short notice, but he had to change places with someone at the last minute. I'll understand if you don't want to do it.'

She thought about it. No matter what their differences were, they had to find a way of working together, didn't they? 'I suppose I could do that.' She just needed a bit of breathing space right now, but she might be feeling more positive tomorrow.

'I'll be in the City in the morning, anyway,' she said. 'My dad asked me to check up on the building work at the property he's renovating while he goes to have talks with his bank manager. I don't mind coming in to work after I've done that.'

'Thanks. I'll book you in.'

Her father's building project was more or less on course, but perhaps that was because he had kept a careful eye on things. He was very clear about what he wanted, and he liked to make sure that everything was going to plan. It was in his nature to do that.

When she looked in on the builders next day, she saw that they had put the last of the partition walls in place, and the electrical work was very nearly finished. The next step would be to bring in the plasterers and arrange for the plumbing to be installed.

On the ground floor, where the restaurant was to be housed, everything was structurally sound and ready for the kitchen equipment to be brought in.

'My dad will be really pleased,' she told the foreman a couple of hours later, as she was about to leave. He walked with her out onto the street.

'Do you think so?'

'Yes…you've done some first-class work here, and you've managed to keep everything pretty much on schedule.'

'We always aim to do a good job,' he acknowledged. 'Not like some I could mention, who try to cut corners.' He inclined his head to indicate a renovation project going on further down the street. 'They landed themselves in trouble again today…some sort of accident with a blowtorch. I heard that there was an explosion. You probably heard the fire engine a short while ago.'

'Yes, I did. I wondered what was going on.' Emma frowned. 'It looks as though the fire crew is still there.'

She knew the firm he was talking about. It was well known that he was locked into a bitter rivalry with a company that was constantly undercutting his prices. They were involved in some building work, converting a property into self-contained apartments, and she took a look at what was going on as she passed by the premises a few minutes later on her way to the tube.

The fire that had been raging for the last half-hour was very nearly extinguished, but apparently the fire officer was still concerned. 'We thought everyone was out of there, but we were wrong,' he told one of his crew. 'I can't think what's keeping the ambulance.'

A police officer came forward and started to move everyone away to the opposite side of the road. 'Stay back, please,' he said. 'We need to bring some equipment through here.'

Threaded through the buzz of talk all around her, Emma heard someone moaning in pain and she looked up at the building, trying to fathom where the sound had come from. The building was wrecked, one side of it open to the elements, and as she stared at the crumbling masonry she was reminded all too vividly of the aftermath of the explosion at her father's restaurant. Fear clamped her stomach. That episode wasn't something that she had ever wanted to revisit.

She hesitated momentarily, her mouth dry, a feeling of terror sweeping through her. The sound of agonised groaning continued, breaking into her thoughts, and she shook off her dream-like state and started to push her way forward through the assembled crowd.

'I'm a doctor,' she said, going over to the police officer. 'Can I help in any way? Has someone been injured?' She was relieved that she had brought her medical bag with her, ready for the afternoon's work. Over the years, she had learned that it helped to be prepared for all eventualities, and she also made a point of keeping equipment to hand in her car.

He nodded. 'Yes, we've a man with burns to his hands and arms, but he's not the only one. It appears that one of the workers was trapped on an upper level—presumably he couldn't escape with the others because of the fire—and then part of the building collapsed. He fell, but landed on a ledge on the next floor. We don't know how badly he's been injured, and we're not sure whether it's safe to move him. They're bringing in a lifting platform so that we can get to him more easily, but there's a concern that the structures above him are still not safe.'

Emma went to attend to the burns patient first of all, covering his wounds with special dressings and setting up an intravenous drip. Then she looked up at the building once more, her heart in her mouth.

'I need to go up there,' she said to the fire officer. 'Can you get me up to the man on the ledge?'

'It isn't safe,' he said. 'I can't allow it, not until we can be sure that we've secured the area.'

'We can't just leave him, not without checking his condition first,' she insisted. Inside, she was shaking, dreading the moment of truth, of facing up to her demons, but she knew that she couldn't leave an injured patient if she had the power to help him. 'A few minutes could make all the difference between life or death or permanent damage, and I need to at least try to take a look at him.'

Still he hesitated, and then she heard Rhys's voice saying, 'I'll go with her. It could be a two-handed job to get him safely down. If you can rig up some sort of board to shield us from the worst of any falling masonry, we'll do what we can to treat him up there and make sure he's safe to be brought down.'

Emma turned to face him, her eyes widening. 'Rhys—what are you doing here?'

'They called the air ambulance because the lunch-time traffic has brought everything to a standstill. The helicopter is the only way to get your patient to the burns unit quickly. They're taking him now, with a crew from the ambulance, and they'll come back for us.'

'I'm glad you're here.' Relief washed over her. Somehow, with Rhys by her side, the operation ahead didn't seem quite so daunting.

He nodded, and then looked up at the collapsed building. 'This brings back memories, doesn't it?' He grimaced. 'But you're right. We can't leave him. A few minutes could make all the difference.'

By now the fire crew had managed to rig up a platform, and the fire chief said flatly, 'You might not get to spend very long up there, and it's going to be tricky. There's not much room to manoeuvre. Bear in mind, we'll pull you out at the first sign of any movement.'

Emma and Rhys were strapped into safety harnesses and then were winched up to the third storey of the building. On a level with the fallen man, they had to negotiate a hastily constructed walkway of planks secured against a joist.

Being smaller and lighter, Emma went first, while Rhys helped to manoeuvre medical equipment and pass it along to her.

She knelt down beside the man, who was obviously in a lot of pain and was becoming agitated. 'I need to get out of here,' he said. 'Why don't they send a fireman? What can you do?'

'I'm a doctor,' Emma said, trying to keep a soothing tone. 'They told me your name is Rob…is that right?'

He nodded, and she added, 'I need to find out where

you are hurt, Rob. Bear with me for a while, will you?' She pulled her medical pack towards her and began to take note of his vital signs. 'Can you tell me if you can feel this…and this?' She checked his reflexes and finally reported back to Rhys.

'His collar-bone is fractured, and his ankle is dislocated,' she said. 'It's cold and discoloured, and there's no pulse. We don't have time to wait to get him to hospital. The ankle needs to be realigned right now so that we can get the circulation back.'

'OK. I'll come and help.' Rhys began to edge his way towards them, and as he did so the stonework beneath them started to crumble.

He stopped, and Emma held her breath. Her heart was pounding. After a moment he adjusted his weight on the planks and began moving towards them once more. This time there was no shifting of the masonry, and Emma set about strapping Rob into a harness, trying to avoid moving his arm so that no stress was put on the collar-bone.

Above them, bits of rubble fell on to the canvas sheeting that had been roughly clamped in place to provide a makeshift shield. Emma shuddered. How long could they rely on it to hold up?

'We'll put the knee in flexion to reduce tension on the Achilles tendon,' Rhys said. 'Then we'll apply traction to the foot while maintaining countertraction to the knee.'

Emma acknowledged that. To Rob, she said, 'I don't understand why you were still up here when everyone else went down to the ground floor at the first sign of a fire. You could have made it to the stairs before this section collapsed, couldn't you?'

In part, she was talking to him, trying to take his mind off the procedure they were trying to enact. Although they had given him a local anaesthetic, it was not an easy manoeuvre.

'I didn't feel well,' he said. 'I think it must have been something I'd eaten. I felt dizzy and sick, and I just couldn't get my head together. I was planning on going home, but the boss had me go up and sort out a fault. He knew I felt rough, but I think he thought I'd been on the booze and it was just an excuse.'

Emma made a face. 'Not your caring, considerate boss, then.'

'Not by a long way.'

Rhys narrowed his eyes as more masonry started to crumble above them. 'We'll mention your sickness to the doctors at the hospital and they'll check you out. In the meantime, we should start trying to get you out of here.'

He immobilised the ankle and then applied a sling to Rob's arm in order to steady the fractured collar-bone. As soon as he had done that, he called to the waiting fire crew.

'We can start to move him out now.' He helped Emma to move back across the planks and onto the platform, and then handed over the medical equipment. 'You go,' he said. 'I'll follow.'

She did as he suggested, and waited for him to descend, too, but he didn't immediately. Instead, he stayed to help the firemen bring Rob down, and she waited, back on firm ground, holding her breath and praying that there would be no more slippage of the fabric of the building.

The press had arrived to capture the moment, and Emma tried to escape, hoping to blend in with the crowd. She didn't want to be subjected to a barrage of questions and find herself in the papers once more.

As soon as Rob was safely down, they transferred him to a stretcher and hurriedly conveyed him to the helicopter. The doors closed, shutting out the rest of the world, and within moments they were airborne.

They went with Rob to A and E. It wasn't their usual procedure, but Rhys said softly, 'We'll grab a drink and something to eat from the cafeteria, shall we? My mouth is dry after all that brick dust. We can be ready to move if James bleeps us.'

He looked at her closely, as though trying to gauge what was going on in her head, but Emma was feeling numb, her mind drifting in a surreal place, trapped in a nightmare of shattered brickwork and broken limbs.

'I don't suppose you had lunch, did you?' Rhys said.

Emma blinked and glanced at the clock on the wall. 'No, I didn't get around to it.' She realised with a sense of shock that the afternoon shift was already drawing to a close. She had been engrossed in Rob's predicament and, perhaps because she had been to her father's place earlier, it had brought memories flooding back...bad memories. Events had taken their toll on her and now she found that she was shaking.

'Dr Benton.' The on-call surgeon touched Rhys's arm. 'May I have a quick word with you about the patient you just brought in?'

'Of course.' Rhys moved to one side, and Emma heard them discussing Rob's medication. The surgeon seemed to be pleased with the way Emma and Rhys had acted to improve the patient's circulation.

'Another collapsed building…you must be getting used to those by now.' A voice cut into her thoughts, scraping along her nerve endings like a knife. She turned and looked into the eyes of the reporter who had been at the boating accident. 'I heard our man escaped with a few broken bones. He told me he hadn't been feeling well before it happened. Something he ate, he said.'

He came and stared her in the face, his manner thrusting, persistent. 'Do you want to add anything to that?'

'No,' she said. 'I've nothing to say.' She turned and started to walk away in the opposite direction.

'Hmm…' He came after her. 'I can understand how you might want to get out of here. There are a lot of sick people about. Some food bug going around, they say. Not pleasant, is it?' His mouth twisted. 'But you'd know all about food poisoning, wouldn't you? What was it at your dad's place? A bad batch of mayonnaise?'

Emma sucked in a quick breath. What was it with this man that he kept following her around, asking questions? Why was he so determined to rake up past history? She wanted to turn around and shout at him, to tell him to leave her alone, but she wouldn't give him the satisfaction of seeing her lose her cool.

He caught up with her and tried to jump in front of her and block her path, but Rhys must have seen what was going on because he quickly ended his conversation with the doctor and moved to waylay him. He said in a grim tone, 'That's enough from you. If I catch you questioning her again, I'll call the police and have you charged with harassment. Stay away.'

The reporter sent him an assessing look. Perhaps it was the steely glint that flared in Rhys's eyes, or maybe it was the rigid set of his shoulders that decided him, but clearly he thought better of getting into an argument with him. He backed down, retreating a fraction, his gaze simmering with the frustration of being thwarted.

'What was all that about?' Rhys asked as they went to buy packs of sandwiches and filled polystyrene cups with coffee to take out from the cafeteria. He clamped lids in place on the cups and took them to the checkout.

'I'm not sure.' Emma frowned. 'I wasn't aware that the food scare was common knowledge.'

He turned his gaze on her. 'What food scare? You're not talking about the people in A and E, are you?' They walked along the corridor towards the lifts.

Emma shook her head. 'No. It was an incident at the restaurant—my father's restaurant—but I don't know how the reporter would have known about that…unless he's been talking to people that my father employed at one time.'

'So there was more trouble with your father's business?'

She pressed her lips together. Was he going to assume

that her father was at fault in everything? She said carefully, 'My dad recruited someone to take over when his first chef was offered a job elsewhere. The *sous* chef wasn't at all happy about that, because he had hoped for the position, and when he didn't get it, we think he started to become sloppy in his work. The new chef and my dad had to speak to him about it on a number of occasions.'

The lift doors opened and they stepped inside. Rhys pressed the button for the top floor.

'One day I sampled some of the mayonnaise that he had prepared, and afterwards I became violently ill—it was lucky that none of the dressing was sent out with the meals, because it turned out that it was infected with salmonella. The *sous* chef was defensive and thought my father blamed him, but he didn't. He simply told him that from then on he was to have the ingredients brought in from different suppliers.'

She glanced up at him. 'I suppose you think we deserve all our troubles, but my dad has always tried to do the right thing. He's a businessman, but he does care about the people around him and he always tried to be an understanding employer.'

Rhys didn't answer. The lift doors opened, and he followed as she walked out onto the roof of the hospital.

'Let's go and sit on Chris's garden terrace,' he suggested, and she acquiesced readily enough, walking with him towards a corner where an assortment of flowering tubs and rustic boxes had been assembled. The copilot was a keen gardener, and he had livened up this tiny area of his workplace with brightly coloured blooms and trellised planters that supported climbing shrubs and served to provide shelter from the breeze.

They sat on the lids of painted wooden boxes that were made for the purpose and which also housed his garden tools. Chris was a perfectionist, and everything was in its place.

Emma opened her lunch wrapping, placing her coffee-cup on the box beside her. 'Thanks for making the reporter back off,' she said, taking a bite of a sandwich and savouring the taste of crispy lettuce and cucumber. 'I don't think he was about to take any notice of what I said.'

'I could see that you were feeling low,' he murmured, swallowing his coffee. 'It must have been difficult for you, going up on to that ledge, knowing that it wasn't safe. I remember how you stayed with Amy when she was injured. You leaned over her to protect her from falling debris, and you did what you could to stem the worst of the bleeding. By the time I arrived there, she was very weak, but I think it was you who kept her going.'

'My father stayed with her, too.'

'Yes, but he felt that he owed it to her, and that it was his duty to be there. You stayed because you hoped you could save her life and you wanted to give her comfort.'

She frowned. 'I don't believe either of us was thinking very clearly. I know that we both wanted to do everything that we could for her.'

Emma lifted her gaze to him, her green eyes troubled. 'It was a dreadful day and now it keeps coming back to haunt us. I don't know why the reporter keeps hounding us this way. What does he hope to achieve?'

Rhys put out a hand and touched the wayward curls at the side of her temple. 'Perhaps he feels rejected. He wanted to get to know you better, didn't he? Only, like the rest of us, you were too busy trying to find a way out of the nightmare.'

Her eyes widened. 'You saw what was going on with him?'

He nodded, his fingers moving to gently tuck the strands of hair behind her ear. She loved the feel of his hand on her face and she savoured the moment. His thumb brushed her cheek, and warmth enveloped her, wrapping itself around her.

He moved closer, his head bent towards her, his gaze focussed on the softness of her lips, and she held her breath, trying to gauge what was in his mind, daring to wonder whether he might be about to kiss her.

'I saw a lot of things very clearly that day,' he said huskily, 'as though time had stood still and encapsulated the moment. You were my sister's best friend and we had all been going around together with a crowd for as long as I could remember, being carefree and having fun, enjoying life simply because we were young and that's what life was all about.'

His mouth straightened. 'But it had to come to an end…there always comes a time when we put our youth behind us and move on. I suppose I had always known that it would happen some day, and I was getting ready to let go…but I just hadn't reckoned on there being such a final moment.'

A line etched its way into her brow. What did he mean? What was he saying? Was he really putting into words what she had known all along? That small crumb of comfort she had briefly tasted was rapidly dissolving on her tongue.

Slowly, he let his hand fall to his side, almost as though he was reluctant to let her go, and then he started to ease back from her.

'Everything changed that day. I wasn't expecting it…none of us were…but it's etched on our minds, in different ways for each one of us, and it seems as if there's no going back.'

Their pagers bleeped in unison, and Emma blinked, checking the gadget at her waist and cutting off the sound with the push of a button. She looked around and tried to take in the reality of where they were. Another call had come in and now they swept into action, brushing aside the debris of their lives.

Rhys didn't care for her, not in the way that she wanted him to care. He had made that all too clear. He was moving on, and if it didn't seem that way in physical terms, most definitely in his mind he had already left her.

CHAPTER FIVE

'CAN you believe this?' Emma's father threw the newspaper down onto the coffee-table and began to pace the floor. 'How did he manage to get hold of the information? It's all there, in black and white for everyone to see…the plans for the new restaurant, the date when we're looking to start up.'

He pressed his lips together in exasperation. 'And then the clincher…all the gory details about a food-poisoning incident, as if that was anything at all to do with our enterprise. No matter that it was a supplier at fault and we nipped it in the bud before there was any problem. Is this reporter trying to finish me off?'

Emma was dismayed. 'It's beginning to look as though he has a problem with us, doesn't it?' Another article…another depressing setback to her father's hopes of making a fresh start. She glanced at him, distressed to see the rigid set of his mouth and the lines of strain that were carved into his face.

From across the room, Kayla looked at him curiously. The little girl was sitting on the rug, playing with the spaniel, but now she asked, 'Are you cross? Have they put your picture in the newspaper? Emma's picture was in there, you know.'

Emma's father glanced at the child. 'I'm sorry, sweetheart. I didn't mean to startle you. No, everything's fine. I think I just need to go and get some fresh air.'

Kayla nodded wisely. 'We do that…Mummy and me. We take Samson for a walk on the common.'

Samson's ears pricked up at his favourite word and Kayla gave him a cuddle. 'I'll take you outside,' she said, glancing at Emma for confirmation.

Emma nodded. 'Don't go beyond the courtyard, though.'

She looked back at her father with affection. He was in his fifties, still a fine-looking man, his eyes the same clear green as her own, though his brown hair was starting to grey a little at the edges now and his shoulders were bent, as though the burden of censure was starting to weigh him down. She could see that the struggle to stay on top of things was getting to be too much for him.

He had worked hard all his life in the construction trade, working overtime in order to build up his finances. He had started with nothing, and everything he had achieved had been brought about by physical effort and sheer determination.

'I should go,' he said. 'I only dropped by to thank you for checking over the building work for me the other day…and I've a thousand other jobs waiting for me.'

Emma laughed and saw him to the door. 'You work too hard,' she said. 'You should try slowing down a bit.'

'That's not really an option,' he murmured, bending to kiss her on the cheek. 'Anyway, you can't talk…this must be the first weekend off you've had in weeks.'

It was an exaggeration, but she was still dwelling on that when she looked out into the street and saw a familiar figure coming towards her. She frowned. What was Rhys doing here?

Her father must have asked himself the same question. He stood very still and Emma heard his swift intake of breath.

'Rhys,' he murmured cautiously as he approached. 'It's good to see you again. It seems to have been a long time since I last saw you…I heard that you and Emma were working together now.'

Rhys nodded an acknowledgement. 'We are, and you're right, it has been a long time.' There was an awkward moment, as both men appeared to be sizing each other up.

Her father hesitated for a second or two, and then asked, 'How is your sister? Is she getting along all right?'

Rhys grimaced. 'I'm afraid not. She isn't doing too well at the moment. She's been depressed for a long time.'

'I'm sorry about that.'

'So am I.'

'It's difficult to know what to do in the circumstances, isn't it? It must be hard for your family.'

Rhys remained silent, and Emma's hopes for any kind of reconciliation between them plummeted.

Emma's father must have sensed that there was no point in prolonging the conversation. He was never going to break through that barrier of resistance. Rhys's family weren't open to any approach after what had happened to Amy.

Instead, he turned to her and gave her a hug. 'I must go. I'll see you next week some time.' He inclined his head towards Rhys, and then walked briskly away.

'I need to go inside and check on Kayla,' Emma said, glancing at Rhys. She still had no idea why he was there. It couldn't be anything to do with work, because he wasn't dressed for it, and he didn't have that brisk, ready-for-anything vibe about him this morning. He was far more laid back.

He looked good—far too good for her peace of mind. He was wearing casual clothes, olive-green chinos that fitted him to perfection, teamed with a dark-coloured shirt. He was tall and lithe, flat-stomached, and altogether he presented a picture that was infinitely pleasing on the eye.

'Kayla?' He lifted a brow in query.

'My neighbour's little girl.' She averted her gaze from his long legs. 'Do you want to come in?'

'Thanks.' Rhys followed her into the living room, and Emma went to make sure that Kayla and the dog were still outside in the courtyard. They were playing a game of tag, the dog jumping up in excitement, while Kayla giggled happily, and Emma smiled, leaving them to it.

'We don't normally see you around these parts,' Emma murmured, going back to Rhys. 'Did you come to see me about anything in particular?'

He shook his head. 'No, actually it was Elliot I came to see.'

Emma frowned. That was odd. 'What makes you think that he would be here?'

'He's not at his own place, and I just wondered if he might have come over to see you. After all, you're only a short walk away from each other. I stopped by on the off chance. Amy was hoping that he would look at some papers, and she asked me to bring them round.'

'Oh, I see.' She didn't, not really, but she was busy fighting off a surge of disappointment at learning that he hadn't come to see her especially, and she was reluctant to dwell on what had prompted him to think that Elliot might be there.

Kayla came in from the courtyard, the dog trailing behind her. 'Hello,' she said, staring up at Rhys. 'Who are you?'

'Hello.' He hunkered down to the child's level. 'I'm Rhys. I work with Emma,' he said. 'I didn't know that she had a little girl. What's your name?'

'I'm not her little girl.' Kayla chuckled. 'I'm Kayla. I live next door with my mummy.' She looked at him as though he might have trouble taking that in and started to explain carefully, 'My mummy works at a chemist's shop, and this is her Saturday for going to work. She doesn't go in every week.'

'Ah…that explains it.' Rhys smiled. 'So Emma is looking after you, is she?'

Kayla nodded. 'Just for a little while. I'm going to my friend's house in a bit, but first we're going to take

Samson for a walk on the common. Emma said so.' She
looked at him as though that point might need clarify-
ing. 'Emma takes him for a walk sometimes when
Mummy's at work, 'cos he needs his exercise, you see,
and Emma says she needs her exercise, too, so she can
keep her tummy flat.'

Emma made a peculiar squeaking sound at that unexpected revelation, and Rhys turned to her in amusement. His glance shifted over her slender shape, gliding
down over the figure-hugging cotton top that she was
wearing and coming to linger on the line of her
smoothly fitting denim jeans.

'Her tummy looks fine to me,' he said. 'In fact, she
looks pretty well perfect all over. I guess she must have
been doing a lot of walking.'

Kayla nodded, wide-eyed, and Emma felt a flush of
heat colour her cheeks. Was he actually saying he liked
the way she looked?

The little girl watched as Rhys stroked the spaniel's
silky ears. 'You can come with us, if you like,' she
added. 'Samson likes you.'

At that moment Samson was jumping up for attention, placing his paws on Rhys's thighs and gazing up
at him with eager expectation. 'See,' Kayla said. 'He
only does that with people he really likes. He growls at
everybody else, or he starts barking, and then Mummy
gets cross with him.'

The doorbell sounded and, as if on cue, Samson
began to bark noisily. Kayla went to fetch her doll from
the settee, and hugged it to her.

Emma went to see who was at the door, and a moment later she came back into the living room, accompanied by Elliot. His visit had taken her completely by surprise, and she was a little subdued, not at all sure what Rhys's reaction might be.

Rhys sent his brother-in-law a narrowed stare. 'I wondered if I might see you here,' he said.

Elliot looked uncomfortable. 'I just brought some croissants back from the bakery,' he murmured, holding out a paper carton. The smell of fresh-baked pastries filled the air. 'They're still warm, and I thought Emma might like to share them with me.' He gave an awkward shrug of his shoulders, as though he didn't quite know how to handle the situation. 'There are enough for all of us.'

Emma wondered if Rhys would refuse the offer and leave, as he had done the other day, but this time he inclined his head and said, 'That would be good. I haven't eaten yet because I was hoping to catch you before you went out.'

'You wanted to see me?' Elliot asked, a line appearing on his brow. Emma left them to talk and went to make coffee in the kitchen at the far end of the room.

'I did. Amy was concerned about some work that you arranged to have done at the house. The workmen arrived and wanted to know a little more detail about what you had planned, but she wasn't sure, so I've brought the papers along with me. Perhaps you could take a look at them? If you want to explain to me, I'll relay the information to the workmen.'

Elliot took the papers that Rhys handed to him and

quickly scanned them. 'Perhaps it would be better if I go and see Amy and explain them myself. We should be able to deal with our problems in an adult manner after all. There's no need for her to contact me through a third party.'

'I'm glad you think so.' Rhys sent him a thoughtful look. 'Obviously Amy must have had second thoughts about that.'

Emma placed butter and pots of fruit preserves on the dining table and set out plates. 'Come and sit down,' she told them. 'Help yourselves to coffee.' She glanced across the room at Kayla. 'There are some buns here for you, Kayla, and some milk.'

Kayla came and sat at the table, breaking off bits of bun and feeding them to her doll.

Elliot started to ask Rhys about his work, and they talked for a while about how Rhys had chosen to work with the helicopter emergency service.

'I didn't want to stay within the confines of a hospital,' Rhys said. 'I felt the need to be out and about, and I wanted the freedom of not having to be in a specific place each day. It makes me feel good to know that by being one of the first to arrive at the scene of an accident, I can make a vital difference to the outcome when someone has been injured.'

'That's what you call life in the fast lane,' Elliot murmured. 'It wouldn't do for me. I'm not sure that I could stand the pace. Lately, things have been crowding in on me, and I've been finding that I need more time to reflect on things.'

'At least you have time for a leisurely breakfast with Emma.' Rhys turned an assessing gaze on him. 'That can't be bad, can it?'

Elliot's mouth made an odd shape. He seemed ill at ease, and he said slowly, 'I've been helping Emma with a problem over her lease. She's applied for an extension and the paperwork was complicated. We're both busy people, but at least this way we get time to talk things through.'

Emma stood up and started to load plates in the dishwasher. Why should Elliot have to explain himself to Rhys? Her lips firmed. Why should she be made to feel that she was doing something wrong by having breakfast with him? Elliot had left his wife, but that was between him and Amy, and it had nothing to do with her. She didn't have any designs on him.

Samson was getting restless. He ran to the door, whining, and Emma said, 'I have to take him out before Kayla's friend arrives to pick her up. I promised Kayla that we would walk across the common.'

Elliot scraped back his chair. 'And I'm supposed to be meeting up with someone in half an hour, so I'll leave you to it, Emma. It was good having breakfast with you. We must do it again some time.'

She nodded and saw him out, and then she went back to the kitchen and finished clearing away. 'Are you going to come with us?' she asked Rhys. 'I've a feeling that Kayla will be disappointed if you don't. She doesn't extend invitations lightly.'

'Then I'd better come along with you.' He smiled at

Kayla. 'I've always wanted a dog of my own, but there's no room for one in my apartment, and I don't have a garden, so he wouldn't have anywhere to run about.'

'Don't you?' Kayla said, looking at him with pity. 'I don't know anyone who hasn't got a garden, except for Mr Marshall at school. Samson loves playing in ours. He likes to dig for stones, and Mummy gets cross because he pulls up the flowers.'

'Oh, dear.' Rhys laughed. 'That's not good, is it?'

Kayla shook her head. By now, Emma had found Samson's lead, and they started out for the common, where the dog could sniff at the shrubbery and inspect each of the trees in turn.

At the far end of the common, there was a brook that meandered and left shallow pools of water when the rainfall was sparse. Ducks were drifting on the water-course, letting the current take them downstream, and Kayla ran towards them. Emma gave her some bread, and they stood for a while, watching as she broke it up into bits and threw it to them.

'I'm sure she thinks you live in a hut of some sort,' Emma said to Rhys. 'Mr Marshall is the school premises officer, and he has his own little shed where he spends most of his time. He likes to potter in there.'

Rhys smiled. 'Well, my place is not quite that bad.'

Emma looked at him. 'You live in the Docklands area, don't you? I heard Martin say something about it to James the other day.'

'That's right, I do. I've been there for about a year now, and I must say I really like it. My apartment looks out over the river, and on a clear day I can see right across London.' He made a face. 'Of course, there are drawbacks to living in an apartment, but it suits my purpose, and it means I'm fairly central for work.'

He sent her an oblique glance. 'Perhaps you should come over and see it one day. I know you like the river, and you might appreciate being able to look out at some of the London landmarks. From my place you can see the boats coming and going to the wharves, and beyond the river to the south there's the nature reserve.'

'It sounds wonderful. I might just take you up on that.' She would like to see his apartment. One thing was for sure, it wouldn't be a cramped little two-roomed place like hers. On the contrary, it was probably quite spectacular.

'It's time that we were setting off for home,' she told Kayla a short time later. 'I expect your friend's mother will be arriving to collect you at any moment. We'd better be ready for her.'

Kayla threw the rest of the bread to the ducks and came back to Emma's side. She slid her hand into Rhys's and danced along between the two of them, without a care in the world.

Back at the flat, Emma let Samson explore the court-yard while she helped Kayla to get ready to go to her friend's house. When the doorbell rang just a short time later, she handed Kayla over to Lindsey's friend.

'Tracey has been really excited about playing with Kayla,' the woman said. 'I'm sure they're going to have a wonderful time—I'll give Lindsey a call when I'm ready to bring Kayla back, shall I?'

'That's a good idea,' Emma said. 'Thanks.' She bent down to give Kayla a hug, but it was a brief embrace because the little girl was already turning excitedly towards her young friend.

'See you, Emma,' she said.

Emma went back inside the flat and gave a Rhys a wry smile. 'It's all go with children, isn't it? They're never still. I don't know if I could keep up if she was my child.'

'I'm sure you would make an excellent mother,' he observed, giving her an oddly quizzical look. 'You're very good with her…and with the dog.'

She chuckled at that. 'I'd better go and bring him in. He's very partial to flowers and I don't think my tubs will stand the attention for very long.'

She went outside to check on him, but a moment later she gave a sharp cry. 'Samson? Oh, no…'

'What's wrong?' Rhys came to stand by her side, and when he saw what she was staring at he said quietly, 'It looks as though he must have eaten something that disagreed with him. Did you leave any food out here?'

'No, of course not. Why would I do that?'

Her heart was beginning to pound. The dog was lying on his side, clearly distressed, and he was panting, with blood coming from his mouth. Close by she could see a black, tarry deposit where he had relieved himself.

'What could have happened to him?' Her voice was thready with shock.

Rhys was looking around the small courtyard. 'You say that you didn't put any food out for him, but there's some meat over there in the corner.' His features were tense. 'From the looks of him, he's been poisoned.'

Emma tried to get her brain back together. 'He's bleeding inside, so that must mean that it's some kind of rat poison. Warfarin—that would make him haemorrhage, wouldn't it?'

Rhys nodded. 'Perhaps we could get some charcoal into him—that would help to prevent any more absorption of the substance. He'll need an injection of vitamin K. That will bring the bleeding under control. We'll have to act quickly…get him to the vet. There's no knowing how long ago he ate the meat, but I'm guessing he must have found it earlier.'

'I don't know how it came to be there.' She frowned, anxiously mulling it over. 'I suppose someone could have gained access from the garden next door. I'm fairly secluded here, but there is a gate, so that Lindsay and I can come around and see one another. I just can't imagine why anyone would do something like this.'

'Perhaps we should think about that later. The main thing now is to do what we can for the dog.'

'You're right.' Emma hurried away to get her medical bag and some bath towels. 'I'll make up a mixture of charcoal, and perhaps between us we can manage to tip it down his throat.' When she came back a minute or so later, she said, 'I've given the vet a call to say that we're on our way.'

They both knelt down beside the dog, and did what they could to get him to take the charcoal. Then they carefully wrapped him in the towels, and Rhys lifted him in his arms.

'If you sit with him in the back of the car, I'll drive,' he said.

Emma did as he suggested. Why would anyone do this? Samson had never hurt anyone. 'I'm just so thankful that Kayla wasn't around to see this,' she said, and then added on a worried note, 'What am I going to say to Lindsey? She thought the dog would be safe with me.'

'It's hardly your fault,' Rhys said. 'How were you to know that someone would do something like this?'

Emma was thinking hard about that. 'I thought someone was hanging around outside a few days ago…there were noises, sounds of scuffling, but we never saw anyone. I wonder if whoever did this thought that Samson was my dog?'

Rhys didn't answer, but she knew that it was a definite possibility. Soon, though, there was no time to dwell on the matter, because they arrived at the vet's surgery, and Rhys gently carried the dog into the treatment room.

'Did you bring the food with you?' the vet asked, and Rhys nodded.

'I brought what was left of it.'

'Good. We'll get it tested, but from the look of him I think you're probably right.' He glanced at Emma. 'It does look like warfarin poisoning. If so, we'll treat him with injections of vitamin K, and I think he might need a blood transfusion at some point. Whatever happens, we'll keep him here and look after him. Most likely he'll be with us for a few days, but with luck he'll make a complete recovery. Usually we continue with the vitamin K in tablet form for several weeks, to make sure that there's no relapse.'

'Thank you. I know Lindsey will be glad to know that he's in safe hands.'

She stroked Samson's head, and then she and Rhys left the surgery. 'There's only one good aspect to all this,' she said, 'and that's the fact that Lindsey has insurance. I daren't even think what the vet's bill will come to.'

They walked back to Rhys's car. Emma was feeling very strange, disorientated almost. 'Thank you for coming with me,' she told Rhys. 'You were brilliant. You didn't hesitate. I was completely thrown by what happened.'

'I was glad to be able to help out,' he murmured. He gave her a wry smile. 'This is turning out to be a very strange day off.'

Just minutes later, though, things became even more out of the ordinary. Emma's phone bleeped, and Rhys's ring tone sounded almost simultaneously.

Emma took the call, and began to frown. 'There's been an accident at the train station,' she said. 'They're calling for people to go in and help out. An express derailed near the tube, and there are multiple casualties.'

'Are you going in?' he asked. 'Shall I turn the car around and head for the City?'

'Yes…I can't just ignore it. I have to do something.' She sent him a sideways glance. 'I take it you're going to help out?'

He nodded. 'Like I said, this day is just totally bizarre.'

They were at the station within a few minutes, and Emma was appalled at what she saw. The rear carriage of an express train had come off the rails and careered into a wall. There must have been some sort of fire, too, because people were walking about with blackened faces and smudged clothes, and one or two had blood coursing from head wounds or injuries to their extremities. Firemen were doing what they could to free people from the wreckage and everywhere there was noise and the overwhelming chaos of destruction.

'Do we know what caused the derailment?' Rhys asked one of the fire officers.

The man shook his head. 'We're not sure at the moment, but witnesses have talked about an obstruction on the line, and it seems that the train was going at such a speed that nothing could be done to avoid it.' He grimaced. 'We're doing what we can to move passengers away from the area—those that can walk. Some others are trapped in the overturned carriage. It's going to take hours to get them all out.'

'Can we get in to treat any of them? Is it safe for us to go to the people who are trapped? I don't mind for myself, but I can't risk my colleague's safety.'

Emma's brow furrowed. 'I wouldn't be here if I wasn't prepared to go and do what I can.'

'Maybe, but you're my responsibility. I'm your boss, and I have to assess the risks. I'm accountable.'

'Not today…we're off duty, remember?'

The fireman led them over to the train. 'We've managed to shore up one part of the carriage. I'll take you there.'

Rhys assessed the situation and looked as though he might stand in her way, but Emma went around him and began to crawl into the shattered compartment, making her way through crumpled metal and treading over broken glass to get to the man who was trapped in there. He was still conscious, but he was in a desperate condition, crushed by the framework of the carriage and with obvious injuries to his upper extremities. He managed to tell her that his name was Callum.

She quickly checked his airway, breathing and circulation, and intubated him, putting in a cuffed endotracheal tube and making sure that he had an adequate supply of oxygen. He was bleeding profusely, and she attempted to stem the flow with a pressure bandage.

'Callum, I'm going to set up two intravenous lines, so that I can give you fluids and something to relieve the pain.'

He nodded, and she turned around to see if Rhys was close by. She thought she had heard him following her and, sure enough, he was attending to a burns patient, removing the man's constricting clothing and running saline over the damaged skin.

'Rhys, I think I'm going to need some help here,' she said quietly. 'I'm not going to get adequate pain relief for him without putting in a supraclavicular block and peripheral nerve blocks. Do you think you could help me with that?'

'Yes. Just give me a minute to dress these burns.' He was already administering crystalloids to his patient and making him as comfortable as possible.

After a moment, he turned to Emma. 'What are we dealing with here?'

'Crush injuries—I've not made any attempt to reduce the fractures and dislocations, but I want to immobilise them so that we can get him out of here. He's going to need more than the usual painkillers for that.'

Rhys nodded, and indicated to the fire crew that they could start to take his patient out. He worked with Emma over the next few minutes to anaesthetise Callum and make his pain more bearable. It was difficult, working in these cramped conditions, but knowing that Rhys was by her side made things seem far less fraught for Emma.

As soon as they were finished, Emma told the crew that her patient, too, was ready to be taken to hospital.

She waited with Rhys as Callum was transferred to a stretcher. The man would have to go straight to surgery and over the coming weeks he would need multiple skin grafts and intensive care.

Carefully, the emergency services worked to remove the patient from the wreckage and transport him to an ambulance that was standing by. It was a tricky operation, because the carriage they were in was being supported by equipment that had been put in place for the purpose, and as they were taking him out through the narrowed entrance, there was a groaning of metal and the carriage gave a sudden lurch.

Emma was thrown sideways and would have hit her head on a mangled seat if it hadn't been for Rhys's swift action. He lunged forward and grabbed her, his hands cupping her arms, pulling her to him and sheltering her against his chest. Debris showered down over them, but he covered her head with his hand and held her to him.

When everything was still once more, he gently eased his grip on her and asked softly, 'Are you all right?'

She looked up at him, her heart hammering, her limbs trembling. 'Yes, I am, thanks to you. Did you get hurt…was there any glass in the fall? You're not cut, are you?'

'I'm fine.' He gazed into her eyes, as though he would search out any hidden pain. 'I thought you were going to smash into the seat. I couldn't bear to think of you hurting yourself. Are you sure you're all right?'

'I'm OK. I just banged my arm against the side of the carriage, but there's no harm done. You stopped me from crashing into it.'

'I'm glad.' He was still gazing down at her, his grey eyes searching her face with brooding intensity, and it occurred to her that by now she should be calming down, getting back on to an even keel, but instead her pulse had quickened even more, and her nervous system was making chaotic leaps as though it was under siege.

Perhaps he sensed her vulnerability, because his head lowered, bringing him even closer to her, his glance lingering on the soft fullness of her mouth.

Her lips parted in heady expectation. He was going

to kiss her. She knew it, and she wanted it, and she closed her eyes in breathless anticipation, so that when his mouth brushed hers, the tantalising sweep of his lips brought a husky sound of urgent need to break in her throat.

He deepened the kiss, tasting the honeyed sweetness of her mouth, drawing from her all the pent-up longing that she had tried to quell.

His heart was thudding heavily, along with her own. She could feel it, even as he moved to draw her into the shelter of his arms, and the blood raced through her veins in a wave of dizzying excitement. His mouth pressured hers and her whole body trembled in aching response.

Then, too soon, he started to draw back, reluctantly easing himself from her, and she looked up into his eyes and saw a glimmer of some dark emotion there. Was he already regretting their quiet moment of intimacy?

'I'm not sure what came over me,' he said in a thickened voice. 'I thought you might have been hurt, but even so…it should never have happened. Perhaps it's all down to this weird, overwrought situation.' He shook his head, as though to break lose any vestige of madness that might attempt to cling on.

He moved away from her, distancing himself as if that would emphasise the point, and she was chilled by the sudden loss of that warmth and closeness that had been so precious, and so very short-lived.

Emma gazed at him in bewilderment. He didn't want

her...of course he didn't want her. What had possessed her to think that anything might have changed?

She might have known that there was never any chance of regaining the empathy and easy familiarity that they had once shared. The barriers would always be there between them, wouldn't they?

CHAPTER SIX

'ARE you both all right in there?' The fireman's voice reached Emma, jolting her out of her stunned introspection. Her mind was racing, her defences thrown into chaos by what had just happened between her and Rhys. She could still feel the imprint of his kiss on her lips, and she wanted to keep it there for all time. The knowledge that he was already regretting it only served to make her more confused than ever.

Rhys answered for her, saving her from having to find the words. He, at least, was functioning properly. 'Yes, we're fine… But what happened to the man you were taking out—and to the fire crew? Is everyone OK?'

'We got him out just in time. We're all doing great.'

'That's a relief.' Rhys was thoughtful. 'I'm going to try to move further along the carriage. I think there's someone trapped just up ahead of us.'

As he spoke, Emma became aware of an odd groaning sound that was coming from somewhere in the distance. She tried to focus her attention on it, to make sense of where it was coming from, but there was a lot of noise going on all around and it was difficult to pin it down.

'Take it slowly,' the fireman advised. 'We've managed to shore things up again at this end, and we're doing what we can to keep things steady, but there could be isolated hiccups. At the first sign of trouble, be sure to stop and stay still.'

'I will.' Rhys turned to Emma. 'Perhaps you should go back and supervise the transfer of patients to the ambulance.'

Emma shook her head. 'I don't think so. I've already passed on the relevant information to the paramedic. I'm coming with you. We don't know what we're dealing with yet.'

'That's why I'm suggesting that you should go back,' he said drily. 'We've already had one scare, and there's no point in both of us taking risks.'

She wasn't going to be fobbed off that way. Her mind and body were back on course, and professionalism was taking over once more. 'You're wasting time,' she murmured. 'Let's just go, shall we?'

He must have seen that there was no point in continuing the argument, because he began to make his way towards the other end of the carriage without further ado. Emma followed, crouching down and moving at a crawl where the twisted metalwork made it difficult to proceed. The sound of groaning gradually became louder.

There were two people at the end of the carriage. One was a man who appeared to be dazed, and he was hunched over, holding his arm and moaning with pain. Emma guessed that the arm was broken.

Rhys knelt down beside him, while Emma went to help a woman who she could see was pinned beneath the corner of a seat. The woman's face was turned away from her, a cloud of hair covering her cheek.

'Let me see if I can get this off you,' Emma said quietly. She struggled for a while, and then Rhys came to lend his support. He must have been taking note of her efforts, watching her while at the same time taking care of his patient. She was glad of his help. Between them they managed to pull the seat out of the way, and Emma gasped as the woman turned towards her.

'Lindsey...' She stared at her friend.

'You know her?' Rhys asked, his dark brows coming together in a straight line.

Emma nodded. 'She's my neighbour...Kayla's mother.'

She turned back to Lindsey. 'It never occurred to me—I had no idea that you would be on this train—but, of course, I should have known that you would be setting off for home round about now.' She tried to gather her wits and act in a manner that was in accordance with her training. 'Don't worry, we'll take care of you. I just need you to tell me where you feel any pain. Can you do that?'

Seeing that she was able to cope with the medical side of things, Rhys went back to his patient.

'It's so good to see a familiar face,' Lindsey said, her tone distracted. 'It's been awful, just lying here, and it feels as though I've been stuck here for ages. I was beginning to despair that anyone would come and find us. I could hear that man—I knew he was in pain but I couldn't get up to go and see how he was doing.'

'He'll be all right,' Emma murmured. 'Rhys is taking care of him. We should concentrate our attention on you. Are you in any pain at all?'

'It hurts just here,' Lindsey said, pointing to the middle of her abdomen, and Emma nodded.

'Anywhere else?'

Lindsey shook her head. 'I'm OK. I just couldn't move because of the seat weighing me down.'

Emma made a swift examination. There was no noticeable injury, except for some clear marking where the seat had been in contact with Lindsey's abdomen. 'We'll try to get you out of here,' she told her friend. 'It'll just take a minute or so until we can get a stretcher through here.'

'I think I can walk,' Lindsey said. 'I'll try, at least. It's not too bad, really.' She made to get up, but Emma gently pressured her back down.

'That's not an option. We need to get you to hospital, so that you can be checked over properly. Even if you think you feel fine, we need to be sure that we haven't missed anything.'

A short time later, they managed to get Lindsey and her fellow passenger out of the carriage. From there they were trundled towards a waiting ambulance.

'How is she?' Rhys asked.

'I don't think she's doing as well as she makes out,'

Emma told him. 'She's concerned about getting back for Kayla, of course, but her pulse is too rapid, and her blood pressure is falling. There's something about her condition that bothers me, and I shan't be happy until we get her looked at properly. I'm worried in case there's any internal bleeding—but she'll need a CT scan if we're to find out exactly what happened.'

'Do you want to go with her to the hospital?'

Emma nodded, but she was frowning. 'I do, but it all depends how badly I'm needed here.'

'I don't think that will be a problem. We seem to have plenty of medical people around now. You go with your friend. I'll catch up with you later.'

Emma could see that more doctors had joined the rescue effort, and she hurried away. If Lindsey was left to her own devices, it wouldn't be beyond her to try to persuade the trauma team that she was fit to be sent home, and even though Emma knew that the team wouldn't simply take her word for it, she wanted to be at Lindsey's side to make certain that all was well.

'They say that I need to go for surgery,' Lindsey said an hour or so later. 'For an exploratory procedure.' Her mouth drooped. 'I don't see the point.'

They were in the emergency room back at the hospital, and by this time Rhys had come along to see how things were going. He had checked up on the patients that had been brought in, and now he came to stand with Emma by Lindsey's bed.

Lindsey looked from one to the other, her features tense. 'Surely I'm just a little bruised, aren't I? The first doctor even said that he didn't think there was too much wrong with me. I'll be fine if I rest, won't I?'

'That was before your CT scan,' Emma explained. 'It turns out that your pancreas was crushed—and there is some evidence that you might be bleeding inside.'

Lindsey frowned, and Rhys said quietly, 'You're very fortunate that Emma insisted on thorough checks. Sometimes a pancreatic injury might be missed when people come into hospital because they are difficult to diagnose, and they can be very dangerous if left. In your case, the surgeon will work to put things right.'

'Depending on what he finds, he'll resection the damaged area, or he might put in a drainage tube to relieve any problems. Either way, you'll need to be monitored over the next few days.' Emma hesitated, waiting for Lindsey to absorb that.

'Days! I can't do that… I need to get back home—there's Kayla and Samson to think about.' She struggled to get her words out. 'I can't just stay here. Her father won't be back for a week or so yet.'

'I'll try to get in touch with him for you, and see if he can come back earlier. I can't see him wanting to stay away while you're in hospital—and in the meantime I'll take care of Kayla and Samson for you.' She winced inside, remembering Samson's particular problems. This was hardly the time to tell Lindsey what had happened to him. She only hoped the poor dog would recover from the poisoning.

'Just you do as the doctors tell you, and try to get some rest,' Emma murmured. 'I'll go and make sure that

Kayla is all right, and we'll both come and visit you tomorrow, I promise.'

They left Lindsey a short time later, and Rhys said, 'I'll take you home, if you like. Do you want to pick up Kayla on the way?'

'That would be good…are you sure?' It would be a relief to get out of there, to begin to put this awful day behind her. 'I don't want to put you to a lot of trouble.'

'I'm sure.' His mouth made a wry twist. 'Besides, the train schedule is all over the place, and I don't think you want to be hanging around for very much longer. I think you must have had quite enough for one day.'

It was true enough, and she appreciated having him take the burden from her. His car was ultra-luxurious, with a soft, cushioning interior that allowed her to sit back and relax on the journey.

Or, rather, it would have been restful, if she hadn't been quite so conscious of Rhys's nearness, of his long legs stretched out to manipulate the foot controls, of his strong hands taking easy but firm control of the wheel. She recalled how those hands had held her close to him not so very long ago, and the memory sent the blood fizzing through her veins.

It wouldn't do for her to dwell on that, though, would it? She looked away and tried to simply focus on the passing scenery.

They picked up Kayla from her friend's house, and when Emma explained what had happened to Lindsey, Tracey's mother was shocked.

'I could help out with Kayla until Lindsey's well

again, if you like. It will be easy enough for me to pick her up from nursery school and keep her with me until you get home from work.'

'Would you? That would be wonderful, thanks.' Emma smiled at the woman, grateful for the offer of a helping hand.

Kayla was aware that her mother was in hospital, but Emma had been careful to shield the little girl from the exact details of what had happened to her.

'When will I see Mummy?' Kayla asked, as they set off for home. She was clearly unhappy about the situation, and was watching Emma intently from the back seat of Rhys's car.

'Tomorrow, all being well. I'll take you to the hospital to see her.'

Kayla relaxed a little and turned her attention to Rhys. 'Are you going to come in the house with us? You can play with Samson. He likes you.'

Rhys pulled in a quick breath, glancing at the child in the car's rear-view mirror. 'Actually, Kayla, Samson has a poorly tummy as well, and he's had to go to the dog hospital, so that the vet can make him better.'

Kayla frowned, and her bottom lip started to tremble, but Rhys said quickly, 'Perhaps we can buy him a soft toy, so that when he comes home he'll have something to cuddle up to in his bed.'

Kayla gave that some thought and then nodded. 'And I'll make a card for Mummy, and pick some flowers for her. She'll like that.'

'That's a good idea,' Rhys murmured. 'You're

right…I'm sure she'll love to have some flowers. I expect they will make her really happy.'

As soon as they reached her flat, Emma set out some biscuits and milk on the table for Kayla and provided her with paper and tissue, along with some glue, so that she could start to make a card for her mother. While the child was occupied, she rang the vet to find out how Samson was doing, and then she made coffee for herself and Rhys.

'How is he?' Rhys asked.

'He's very poorly. They've confirmed that it was warfarin on the meat, and they're treating him specifically for that. It's too early to say how he's going to fare, but they're doing their best to make him as comfortable as possible.'

Her heart was heavy, and her mind was churning with questions as to why the dog had been singled out this way. She handed Rhys a cup of coffee and went to gaze out of the French doors at the little courtyard.

'I can't think who would have wanted to poison the dog,' she said, keeping her voice low so that Kayla wouldn't hear. 'I know he could be noisy, with his barking, but it never really bothered me. I know most of the people who live around here,' she said. 'I just can't believe that any of them would do something like this.'

Rhys frowned. 'Even so, you should take extra care if there's someone unstable hanging around. Make sure that you lock all your doors, and push the bolts home.'

She turned to him, her eyes cloudy with distress. 'Do

you think all this could have been aimed at me? It's true that I often take Samson out for walks—and whoever did this might have thought that he was my dog. Perhaps it wasn't Samson who was the real target.'

Rhys made a grimace. 'Are you wondering if it's possible that someone might bear you or your family a grudge?'

She nodded, but couldn't bring herself to put her fears into words.

'It's a fact that there have been all those stories in the newspaper, stirring things up, and I suppose you could be right. After all, people were hurt in the explosion at the restaurant—perhaps someone feels that your father shouldn't be starting up in business again.'

She stared at him, the colour rapidly leaving her face. 'Do you really think so?'

He watched her steadily. 'I know that my own parents have put in an objection, and I doubt they can be alone in their feelings on the matter. It's not what you want to hear, but it was always on the cards that people might not be happy to have him granted a licence to start up another restaurant. What is there to say that he will follow health and safety procedures any better this time?'

Emma was disturbed to find that she was shaking inside. 'Surely no one would be this vengeful?' she managed, but in her heart she knew that there might well be something in what he was saying. She said haltingly, 'How can I prove that he wasn't responsible? No one is prepared to listen to anything we say.'

She didn't really expect him to answer. Even Rhys stood against her father…Rhys, whom she had known for years.

He said carefully, 'I suppose if you want to go down that route, you would have to think about who was working in the restaurant that day, and ask yourself whether anyone would have borne him a grudge…or perhaps there was some rival who wanted to see him go out of business. Whose purpose would it have served to have him closed down?'

She looked at him afresh. Was he really offering advice, helping her to find a way to resolve this situation? A small ray of hope sprang to life inside her. Perhaps he was not so set against her family as she had believed.

She said, 'There could have been any number of workers who didn't make the grade, over time. My dad did what he could to make sure they had the right training and he was keen to show them how things should be done, but there were always those who fell by the wayside. As to that particular day, I must say I don't think there was anyone there who wasn't a solid part of the team.'

Rhys's shoulders lifted a fraction. 'Perhaps you should give it some more thought…but not right now. After all, you were supposed to be off duty today, but you've been kept very busy, with very little time to yourself, and your nerves have been stretched to the limit. It might help if you sleep on it. You might be able to come up with something if you approach the matter with a fresh mind.'

He looked at her searchingly. 'You're off duty tomorrow, aren't you? Maybe you'll have an easier day. Take the pressure off yourself and things might become clear.'

She nodded. 'Perhaps you're right. Is that what you're planning to do? You're not due to go to work either, are you?' She was wondering what had provoked his change of heart. Up to now he had been so much on the side of his family in all this, and now he was actually considering that she might have a point.

'I said that I would go to see my parents, and have lunch with them. My father wants some help with landscaping the garden. He planned on doing some of the work himself, rather than get people in. He thinks it will be a challenge, and good exercise for him.'

'That sounds very much like hard work to me.' She added thoughtfully, 'Actually, I'll probably have just as full a day tomorrow. After I've been to see Lindsey at the hospital, I might take Kayla to the park—Regents Park, probably, so that we can go and see the animals at the zoo. We could have a picnic and it might help to take her mind off things.'

'That sounds like a good idea.' He glanced towards the door and said, 'I should go.'

He seemed to hesitate, but then he reached for her and lightly brushed her cheek with his hand, so that her glossy curls shifted and quivered with the movement. Her skin was warmed by his touch, and tingled in response as his fingers traced the line of her cheekbone and moved to shape her jaw.

In that moment he made her feel cherished, as though he was reluctant to take his leave of her, but she knew that she must have been imagining things. It was just a friendly gesture, wasn't it? It meant nothing.

'Take care,' he said softly, 'and remember what I said about being sure to lock up…even when you're in the house. It's just a precaution, but you don't want someone sneaking in off the street.'

'I will.' She saw him out of the apartment and then went back inside to help Kayla with her card. She felt strangely detached, as though part of her was missing now that he was gone, and her world was in a state of turmoil.

The next day, she took Kayla to see her mother in hospital, and afterwards the little girl was subdued, much as Emma had expected. Lindsey was feeling the after-effects of surgery, and she was sore and uncomfortable, though she was relieved to see her daughter.

'How are you?' Emma asked.

'I'm OK. The surgeon told me that I was lucky,' Lindsey said with a wry smile. 'He says my pancreas was crushed and damaged, but he should be able to save it. He put in a drainage tube, as you said he might.'

'Are you going to come home soon?' Kayla asked.

'In a few days, all being well,' Lindsey told her.

Kayla looked with curiosity at her mother's various intravenous lines and drips. 'Do they hurt?'

'No. The doctors put them there so that they can give me medicine through them to make me feel better, and so that they can give me food and water that way. I'm not allowed to eat anything until my tummy's better.'

The child looked at her doubtfully. 'I'd rather eat with my mouth.' Then she brightened up, and added, 'We're going to the park. Emma's brought a picnic, and we're going to look at the animals in the zoo and then we're going to sit and eat the food. She's made some jelly, and I'm going to have ice cream as well.'

Lindsey smiled. 'It sounds as though you're going to have a lovely time,' she said, putting an arm around the little girl and giving her a kiss.

They left her to rest, and made their way to the zoo. It was a relief to find that Lindsey was recovering after her ordeal, and Emma had managed to hedge around the question of Samson and his welfare, still not wanting to burden Lindsey with the worry. Luckily Kayla had been distracted by the upcoming visit to the park and had made no mention of him.

A couple of hours later, after Kayla had excitedly explored the various animal compounds, Emma was more than ready for a break and something to eat.

'Shall we find a place to sit down and go and have our picnic?' she asked.

Kayla was happy to agree to that, and after scoffing a selection of ham, egg and cheese sandwiches, along with banana, jelly and ice cream, she was ready to go on. 'I want to see the bird house,' she said.

Some time later, when she had seen everything that there was to see, Emma suggested that it was time to go home. 'We'll walk back to the tube station at Camden Town.'

Kayla danced along beside her, thrilled with the day's

activities. 'Can we go and see Mummy again?' she asked. 'I want to tell her all about it.'

'Yes, tomorrow,' Emma said. They were walking by Primrose Hill, heading towards the station, when she heard someone calling after them. Turning, she was startled to see Elliot walking towards her. 'This is a surprise. What are you doing around here?' she said.

'I've just been to see Amy,' he told her. 'We have a place not far from here.'

'Oh, yes, of course. I forgot.' She recalled Rhys telling her that they had moved to a stylish duplex flat. Apparently, it was spacious and light, and had a lovely garden, but it wasn't likely that Emma would ever be invited there as a welcome guest.

Elliot paused, looking at Kayla and giving her a smile. 'It looks as though you've been having a good time.' He glanced at the stuffed toy she was holding. 'Did you buy that monkey at the zoo?'

Kayla nodded. 'It's for Samson, when he gets back from the vet.'

'Oh, I see.' He didn't, but it didn't appear to bother him. He touched Emma's arm in an affectionate gesture. 'My car's not far away—are you heading for home? I can give you both a lift.'

'Yes, we are. Thanks, that would be great.' She glanced around. 'Where are you parked?'

'Just along the street a bit. I was just coming out of a shop, and I was going to get into the car and drive off, when I saw you.' He put an arm around her shoulder and turned her in the direction of Primrose Hill. Together, they walked along the road, with Kayla talking animatedly and Elliot laughing at her descriptions of the penguins at feeding time.

'They were really greedy,' the little girl said, 'and they ate the fish straight down.'

Elliot gave Emma a sideways glance. 'It sounds as though you've had a full day.'

She smiled at him. 'That's true enough.'

The journey home didn't take long, and he dropped them off at the flat, turning down Emma's offer of coffee. 'I have to go and sort out these plans for the workmen and give them a call,' he said. 'We were having the kitchen redesigned before we split, and I suppose we need to go ahead with it.'

'OK.' Emma went inside the flat. She thought of setting Kayla down to play with her toys while she got on with a few chores, but the child was yawning, and so she laid her down in the bedroom for a nap instead.

By the time the doorbell sounded a few minutes later, Kayla was fast asleep. Emma went to answer the door, guessing that Elliot might have changed his mind and returned, but it wasn't Elliot who stood there.

'Rhys? I thought this was your day off. Weren't you planning on going to visit your parents?' Seeing him standing there had thrown her completely off balance.

He inclined his head in agreement. 'Yes, that's true. I've been to see them.' He sent her an up-and-down look, taking in the line of the denims that clung faithfully to her shape and pausing to dwell on her soft curves that were draped by the loose over shirt that she was wearing. 'Aren't you going to invite me in?'

'Of course.' She stepped back to let him into the hallway. 'I wasn't thinking.'

'No.' He looked at her oddly. 'I did wonder about that.'

'Come through to the living room,' she said. 'We'll have to be quiet, because Kayla is asleep in bed. She's exhausted after her busy day.'

'I can imagine.'

She stared at him, drinking in his long-limbed frame, hardly able to take in the fact that he was actually there. He was wearing dark trousers that drew her gaze to his muscled thighs and a casual shirt that was cut from fine linen, open at the neck to reveal the lightly bronzed column of his throat.

'Were you expecting to see Elliot again?' she asked. 'He was here, but he's gone back to his own place.'

His gaze narrowed on her. 'No, actually, I came to see you. I brought a safety chain for your door. I thought I would fit it for you if you agreed to it.'

She frowned. 'You're serious, aren't you…about this threat of someone hanging around?'

'I am. Anyone who would think of poisoning a dog has to be treated with caution. We don't know what he's capable of.' He studied her, and she wasn't sure what lay behind his intent scrutiny. 'Shall I go ahead and fit it for you?'

'Yes…please, go ahead, if you don't mind doing it for me.' She hesitated. 'Can I get anything for you—a drink, a sandwich?'

'Nothing, thanks. I've eaten.'

There was something about his manner that gave her pause for thought, but she couldn't quite figure it out, and she reconciled herself to simply watching him work. The job didn't take long. He had brought with him a drill and all the tools that he needed, and within a very short time the safety chain was in place.

'That should keep things secure,' he said after a while, putting down his tools and surveying his handiwork.

She leaned back against the doorjamb, letting her glance trail over him. 'I didn't realise how much I was bothered by what has been going on,' she murmured, 'but I feel so much safer now. I don't know how I can thank you.'

He sent her an oblique glance, his mouth tilting in an intriguing fashion. 'I could think of one or two ways,' he murmured. His gaze drifted over her, gliding over her soft curves, and there was a glint in his eye that sparked off a thrill of response in her.

She wasn't at all sure that she knew what was going on here. 'Really?' she said huskily. 'Perhaps you should enlighten me.'

It seemed that he was only too ready to oblige. He moved towards her, taking his time, closing in on her until he was standing in front of her, and already she was wondering if she would come to regret her foolhardiness. By now, though, it was way too late to take back the words.

He slid his arms around her waist, his gaze settling

on the fullness of her mouth. His body lightly pressured hers, and then he bent his head, swooping down to claim her lips. His kiss was gentle, but thorough, and he tantalised her, taking her breath away with his smooth expertise. She had never experienced a kiss quite like this before, but one thing was for sure…he was a man who knew exactly what he was doing.

He deepened the kiss, drawing her to him so that his thighs were against hers and her limbs became weak, boneless. Her whole being was taken up with an overwhelming need for him. Hadn't she waited a lifetime for him to kiss her and hold her like this?

He shaped her with his hands, arousing every nerve fibre in her body, bringing her senses to clamouring life. She was feverish, her blood turning to flame, and recklessly she moved against him, desperate for his touch, aching for the feel of his body against hers. For a breathless moment it occurred to her to wonder how she had survived for so long without losing herself in his arms and giving herself up to the thrill of this heady delight.

Perhaps she had even said it aloud, because he murmured softly against her mouth, 'Tell me what it is that you want… Shall I touch you here…or here? Is that better?' His hand covered her breast momentarily, and then his thumb traced the hardened nub and circled, leaving a path of fire in its wake.

'Is that what you want?' He kissed her again, a demanding, possessive kiss, his lips enticing a trembling response.

She didn't answer him. She couldn't, not right at that moment. Her mind was somewhere else, lost in a world where common sense had no existence. Something was bothering her, though, tugging at the outer reaches of her sensibilities.

'I can give you everything you need,' he said, his voice roughened. 'Believe me. You only have to say the word.' He looked into her bemused eyes and smiled. 'You look dreamy and bewildered all at the same time. What's troubling you?'

He was right in thinking that something was amiss, but her thoughts were too fragmented for her to be able to put them into words. She simply didn't understand how an experience that was so heavenly could be in any way wrong.

Somehow, she managed to find her voice. 'Just yesterday you were telling me that you shouldn't have kissed me,' she said on a ragged note, 'and now everything seems to have changed. I'm not sure that I know what's going on. Perhaps I'm not ready for any of this. I have to take time to think things through.'

'Why do you have to do that?' His arms closed around her, drawing her to him once more. 'Are you really so taken up with Elliot that you can't see how things could be between you and me?'

'Whoa…wait a minute.' She put the flat of her hand on his chest, pushing him away a little. 'What do you mean? What does Elliot have to do with any of this?'

'I saw you with him this afternoon, when you were coming from the park. You can't deny that you were together. I was on my way to see Amy, and I saw you.

He had his arm around you and you made a very cosy trio.'

He gazed down at her, his glance lingering on the softness of her mouth. 'He's married, Emma. You have to remember that. He's not for you. You should concentrate your attentions on someone who's available, someone who doesn't have any ties.'

She stared at him, light dawning in her eyes. 'Is that what this is all about?' she said, her mind whirling. 'You think that I'm involved with Elliot?'

'I don't see any logical reason why he should have left Amy. I know they both say that things have gone wrong between them, but Amy has her doubts. She believes that he has found someone else.'

'And that's why you kissed me, isn't it?' Incensed, she glared at him, her body still reeling from the shock. 'You thought you would entice me away from him and show me that there are other men around.'

His shoulders moved in a negligent shrug. 'It wasn't quite like that…but I'm not married. No one is going to be hurt if you should decide to take up with me.'

If you should decide… The words echoed through her mind. Didn't he know how much he was hurting her with his casual, offhand play for her? She had always wanted him, cared for him, dared to hope that something might come of their relationship, and it was all for nothing, because he was just using her for his own ends, wasn't he? She didn't want him like this.

Emma wriggled away from him, and when he would have come after her she tensed her limbs, throwing up a barrier, every part of her warning him off. 'Don't flatter yourself that I would even give it a thought. What makes you think that you're even in the frame? You caught me unawares, that's all. Believe me, if I was looking for someone, you'd be the last person I'd turn to.'

He sent her a quizzical look. 'This is just a misunderstanding. You're getting yourself worked up over nothing.'

'No, it isn't a misunderstanding. I'm perfectly well aware of what you were trying to do, and I have to tell you that I resent being treated that way.'

She braced herself and faced him squarely. 'I want you to go, now. Please, leave.'

CHAPTER SEVEN

'WE'VE managed to cut her free from the wreckage of the car, Doctor,' the fire officer said, 'so whenever you're ready, you should be able to move in and bring her out.'

'That's good. Thanks.' Rhys turned to Emma and Martin. 'OK, let's get started, shall we? We need to work together on this. The pain medication Emma gave the patient seems to be working, so we'll make a start by immobilising her spine with a backboard. Let's try to get her into the helicopter as smoothly as possible.'

He went over to the car and spoke gently to the injured woman. 'Sarah, can you hear me? Are you with me?'

The woman opened her eyes and nodded slightly, but didn't say anything. She was a slim woman in her early forties, and up to now she had been vague about what exactly had happened to her. Emma was worried about that. All she appeared to know was that she had been driving along and then somehow she had crashed her car.

'We're going to get you out of there now. It looks as

though your hip has dislocated, and there's also a fracture to your leg, so this might be a little uncomfortable for you, but we'll try to get you into a position that will be easier for you to cope with.'

The manoeuvre was a difficult one, but by acting as a team they succeeded in bringing the woman out of the tangled metalwork of the car and then they transferred her to the waiting helicopter. Chris, the copilot, radioed ahead to make sure that a surgeon would be standing by at the hospital to receive her and that a theatre would be made ready.

As they took off, Emma looked back at the place where the road curved slightly and the car had careered headlong into a brick wall. She saw it, but none of it made sense, and she couldn't fathom out quite what was wrong. All day she had been battling with this sense of unreality. It was as though she was empty inside, as though nothing mattered any more.

'You're looking very subdued,' Rhys commented, sending her a sidelong glance. 'What's wrong? Do you think we might have overlooked something, or left some equipment behind?'

Emma lifted her gaze to him. Didn't he ever miss anything? He was obviously keeping a close eye on her. Perhaps her preoccupation was beginning to show, and that wasn't good. It was one thing Rhys taking note, but it wouldn't do for her colleagues to become aware that something was wrong, would it? She was here to do a job of work after all.

The day had not gone smoothly so far. They had

been rushed off their feet, attending to emergencies one after the other, and she had done her best throughout to keep a clear head. It was difficult, though, to go on working so closely with Rhys in a calm and professional manner when her mind was taken up with the way he had kissed her back at the flat. How could he have done that? How could he have shown her the sweet taste of joy, and then let her down so badly, destroying everything?

He didn't seem to be at all fazed by yesterday's events, and that was annoying. It might be perfectly feasible for him to behave as though nothing had happened, but she was finding it far more of a problem.

'I suppose I'm wondering why the accident happened at all,' she said, reverting to safer ground. 'The weather conditions are fine, and there was no dramatic bend in the road, or even a great deal of traffic about. The patient's heart rate is fast, but there's no underlying abnormal rhythm or any sign that points to what might have gone wrong. It all seems very odd.'

'Perhaps she had an argument with her husband earlier, or maybe she was simply distracted.' Rhys watched her in a steady fashion, a faint twist to his mouth. 'It happens sometimes, especially where women are concerned. They seem to be just fine and then they go and get emotional and out of sorts, and all manner of things start to go wrong.'

Her green eyes sparked fitfully. Was that meant to be a dig at her? She glowered at him from under her lashes, but she wasn't going to allow him to provoke her into saying something that she would regret later. If he thought she was emotional and uptight, he would learn that she could just as easily be the opposite. See how he coped with cool and withdrawn. She would teach him that he couldn't make fun of her and get away with it.

She looked away and made an effort to control her breathing. Thank heaven her shift was due to come to an end any time now.

Back at the hospital, she handed her patient over to the surgical team and then went to change out of her uniform. When she went back into the main body of the unit a few minutes later, Rhys was waiting for her.

'Are you planning on going to see Lindsey before you go home?' he asked.

'Yes, that's right.' She would have liked to walk straight past him, but people would have thought that odd. 'Her friend is going to drop Kayla off at the hospital, and I said I would take her to see her mother.'

'Then perhaps I'll walk along with you. I'm meeting Amy at the lift bay downstairs. She has an appointment with a consultant and then she's going on to have tea with my parents.' He frowned. 'The hospital appointments are ongoing. The specialist is trying to find a way to help her to break out of her depression.'

'He doesn't seem to be succeeding very well, does he?'

'No, that's true. No one seems to be able to get at the root cause of her troubles.'

Emma stared at him. Was he actually coming to believe that the accident at the restaurant wasn't the beginning and end of everything?

He walked with her along the corridor. 'I imagine you're going straight home after you've seen Lindsey. It must make things difficult for you, having to cope with a small child, and it must be very limiting if you have to run your timetable around nursery school and so on. Isn't her husband able to get home to help out?'

'Not for a day or two. He's out of the country on business. I think they're having some trouble getting hold of him.' She pulled in a quick breath. 'Anyway, I'm getting by well enough. Kayla's a sweet little girl, and she's no trouble at all.'

She paused, and then added, 'Besides, I don't have to go straight home today. I planned on spending an hour or two in the City first, looking around the shops. There are one or two things I need to buy, so Elliot said that he would call in at the hospital and take over from me.'

She waited a moment to let him absorb that. Already, a small line was digging itself a notch in his brow. 'He has to come by here on his way to meet a client, you see. The girls are going to a birthday party, but Tracey's mother has an errand to do first…it's all a question of timing, really. Elliot said he was going that way and would drop Kayla off at her party so that I could go in the opposite direction.'

She sent him an oblique glance, gauging his reaction to the mention of Elliot's name. If he really thought that she and Elliot were involved with one another, he could think about the arrangements they had made and stew in his own juice for a while. She wasn't about to let him off lightly after the way he had treated her.

His eyes narrowed, but he didn't rise to the bait. 'How is Lindsey doing?' he asked instead.

'She's not doing too badly, I suppose. She was lucky that there were no other injuries, other than a degree of bruising internally. She's being treated for acute pancreatitis, and that means she'll have to stay in hospital for a few days yet. We're hoping that she'll make a full recovery.'

By now they had reached the lower floor of the hospital, and she said, 'I have to go. I can see Tracey's mother waiting for me by the door.'

She walked away from him, and didn't look back, and she didn't much care if he thought her parting from him was abrupt.

Kayla greeted her with a hug. She was overjoyed to be going to see her mother. 'I want her to come home,' she said, 'and I want to see Samson as well.'

'I know you do,' Emma murmured. 'At least they're both feeling a little better now. Perhaps it won't be too long before things are back to normal.'

The visit went well. Lindsey was feeling much stronger, and she had even managed to speak to her husband's boss on the telephone. 'They're doing what they can to find him and bring him back,' she told Emma. 'He's away somewhere, showing a group of Japanese visitors around the various projects, and the boss seems to think they've made a detour somewhere along the way. I thought perhaps they shouldn't try to get in touch with him, but I don't think I'm going to be able to manage too well on my own when I get home—not for a week or so, anyway.'

'You know that I'll do whatever I can to help,' Emma murmured, and Lindsey nodded, giving her an appreciative smile.

They left a while later, when Lindsey started to get tired, and Emma walked with the child to the cafeteria, where she had arranged to meet Elliot.

She was surprised to see Rhys in there, sitting at a table with Amy, and for a moment or two she dithered, wondering whether she ought to leave.

It wasn't her way to turn her back on trouble, though. When she had purchased cake and milk for Kayla, she took her tray and approached them cautiously, looking for a table but glancing at the woman who had once been her friend.

Rhys's sister was attractive, her long black hair plaited into a neat style at the back of her head and pinned up with clips, lending emphasis to the slender line of her neck and the perfect shape of her cheekbones. Her features were strained, though, and she was pale, with shadows beneath her eyes.

'Would you like to join us?' Rhys asked.

Emma hesitated, but then said, 'Thank you. That would be good.' She didn't want to refuse an opportunity to make up with her one-time friend.

Rhys pulled out a chair for her, and another for Kayla, while Emma put down the tray and then searched in her bag for a colouring pad and pencils. She had learned that it was a good idea to be prepared where children were concerned, and now she handed them to the little girl.

'Hello, Amy,' she said with a smile as she sat down. 'I didn't expect to run into you here, but it's good to meet up, isn't it?'

Amy frowned, but said nothing.

Emma tried again. 'It's been such a long time since I saw you last. How have you been getting along?'

Amy still didn't respond, but instead she looked uneasy, drawing back a little. She stared awkwardly at Kayla, a wary look coming into her grey eyes, and Emma realised that she was probably very guarded around children since she had come to believe that she couldn't have any of her own. Perhaps any child served as a reminder of that loss.

'This is my neighbour's little girl,' Emma murmured. 'I'm taking care of her while her mother's in hospital.'

'I see.'

Emma frowned. Amy was monosyllabic and this was turning out to be much more difficult than she could ever have envisaged. She glanced quickly at Rhys, and he said quietly, 'They've just been to see Kayla's mother. She was injured and she's staying on a ward on the third floor. Emma and I went to help her when the train was derailed.'

'I read about that in the papers.'

It was a start. At least she was talking, and Emma said quickly, 'It was a horrible business. Some people were really badly hurt.' Her expression was thoughtful as she looked at Amy, and she asked, 'How are you feeling these days? I know that you've been quite low in yourself, but have you recovered from the physical injuries?'

'I still walk with a bit of a limp,' Amy answered stiffly. 'It seems to be taking a long time for me to get over it.'

'I'm sorry.' Emma frowned. 'I didn't realise that there was any lasting problem. Is there anything that can be done to make things easier for you?'

'I think they've tried everything that there is to try.'

Rhys interrupted at this point, and said, 'Amy is having physiotherapy. There was some scar tissue left after her operation, and the treatment is designed to free everything up.'

Emma nodded. 'These things can take quite some time.' As she said it, she was aware that Amy was looking towards the door of the cafeteria, and now her face had begun to lose what little colour it had had to begin with. She guessed that Elliot had walked in.

Elliot came over to them, and said with a frown, 'I didn't realise that you would be here, Amy. I came to meet Emma. I promised that I would drop Kayla off at a birthday party.' He hesitated, looking uncomfortable. 'How are things? Did you manage to sort out the problem with the workmen the other day?'

Amy's mouth made a straight line. 'You came to meet Emma? How very cosy.' Her shoulders stiffened. 'It turns out that I was right all along, wasn't I? I thought there was something going on.'

He looked at her blankly, and Emma leaned forward and said softly, 'It isn't what you think, Amy.'

Amy directed a laser sharp stare in Emma's direction. 'I wasn't talking to you.'

Taken aback, Emma stared at her, sucking in a sharp breath. Then she collected herself and stumbled to her feet. She was upset, tormented by the scarcely veiled accusation Amy had made, and shocked because of the cold way Amy had spoken to her.

Determined to hide the true extent of what she was feeling, she said in a careful tone, 'Kayla, we should go and wait over by the door. Bring your colouring book with you. I think Amy and Elliot need to talk for a while.' She picked up the child's plate and the half-empty glass of milk and walked away.

There was a table by the exit, and Emma went over to it and sat down, letting Kayla trail after her.

'I haven't finished colouring the teddy bear,' Kayla objected.

'That's all right. Sit down and you can finish it now.'

Rhys came to join them and Emma's brows drew together. 'Doesn't your sister need your support?'

He shook his head. 'You were perfectly right in what you said.'

She sent him a quick glance. Was he giving her the benefit of the doubt, and finally coming to the realisation that nothing was going on between her and Elliot? 'Was I?'

'Yes. She needs to spend some time alone with her husband.'

Emma gritted her teeth. 'Then perhaps I'll give the shopping a miss and take Kayla to the party myself. I just need to call in at A and E before I leave.'

'Why is that?'

Her mouth firmed with exasperation at having to explain herself to him. 'I've been giving some thought to that last patient and the car crash, and I want to have a word with the team that's treating her.'

'Is this to do with the reason for the crash?'

'Yes. When I spoke to the woman first of all, she said something about feeling dizzy and having a headache, but her voice was slurred and I thought it was just that she was confused after the accident. Now I'm beginning to wonder if I heard her right. If she was trying to tell me that she had been suffering from those symptoms for some time before the accident, then it could be that there was a medical cause behind the crash after all.'

He was thoughtful for a moment or two. 'You might have something there. It certainly won't hurt for them to do a neurological work-up on her once she's recovered from the surgery.' He gave her a narrowed stare. 'It just goes to show how your mind keeps ticking over when you're preoccupied with other things, doesn't it? I'm sure you've had lots of unrelated matters to deal with since we handed her over to A and E, but your brain is still busy trying to figure things out.'

'That's true.' She hesitated. 'The same probably applies to you. After all, you're most likely fully aware of what's going on between your sister and Elliot right now, even though you're standing here, talking to me. I know it because I see you looking their way from time to time, and I'm pretty sure that you're taking everything in. Even so, you aren't showing any signs of wanting to go back to help her out.'

'That's because I happen to think that Elliot should stay with her, and if he's going on to visit a client, maybe he could drive her to my parents' house. It won't take him too far out of his way. In fact, I'm going to go over there and suggest it to them right now. You and I could take Kayla to her party and leave them to it. At least it will give us time to talk.'

'I'm not sure that I want to talk to you.'

He made a wry face. 'I do realise that, but I don't think we have any choice if we're to go on working together. We have to find some way of settling our differences.'

She scowled at him. 'Did you plan this when you knew that Elliot would be coming here?'

His mouth firmed. 'No, I didn't, but since they're together and talking to one another, it seems like a good idea.'

'I don't know why I should listen to a word you say, let alone go along with your plans. It seems to me that you're very quick to form conclusions and far too slow to admit that you might have been wrong.'

'If I own up to my faults, will you agree to come with me?'

She wrinkled her nose at that. 'I suppose I could consider it.'

'Then I admit it. I might have been wrong. I jumped in with both feet and drenched us both, and I should have stopped and given it some more thought.'

'Might have been wrong?' She glared at him, but he was already turning away and heading for the table where Elliot and Amy were engrossed in taut conversation.

'That's all settled,' he said, coming back to her a short time later and looking pleased with himself. 'They're going to stay and try to sort things out between them. I told Elliot that you would look after Kayla.'

She glanced back at their table. 'Hmm…I'm not convinced that they will manage to sort out anything. Your sister looks as though she's about ready to blow a fuse.'

His response to that was dry. 'I should imagine Elliot is man enough to deal with that. Shall we go?'

'I suppose so.'

Kayla slipped her hand into Emma's, and together the three of them made their way down to A and E. Emma left Kayla with a nurse while she and Rhys went to check up on their car-crash patient. As expected, she was undergoing surgery, but they passed on their fears about what might have caused the accident to Emma's former boss, the consultant in charge of the unit, and were assured that the matter would be followed up.

'Are we going now?' Kayla asked, beginning to be impatient. 'I want to go to the party. I bet Tracey's there already.'

'We are,' Rhys told her. 'We're going there right now.'

'So where is this party being held?' Rhys asked, turning to Emma as they went out to the car park.

'Kensington Gardens. They're all going to gather outside in the sunshine and enjoy the outdoor activities. There's a huge pirate ship for them to play on, and there are teepees and lots of toys for them to enjoy. I think they're going to have tea in the café later on.'

'Sounds like fun.' Rhys checked that Kayla was settled securely in her seat, and then he drove them to the venue.

The party organiser came to greet them, and after a few minutes Emma said goodbye to the little girl. She gave her a hug and left her in the care of a helper who had been assigned to look after Kayla and Tracey until Tracey's mother was arrived later.

She walked back to the car with Rhys. 'She looks as though she's going to have a good time,' she said.

Rhys nodded. 'I'm sure Lindsey will appreciate that you're making a good job of looking after her.' He sent her a probing glance. 'What does she think about what happened to her dog? I take it you've told her all about it by now?'

'Yes, I've told her. I had to wait until she was stronger in herself, but she took it quite well. Of course, it helped to be able to tell her that he was on the mend.' Emma paused. 'She can't think of any reason why anyone would want to do that to Samson.'

'You didn't ever believe that it was anything to do with Lindsey, did you?'

Emma shook her head. 'No, I didn't. I think it's more likely that it has something to do with the stories that were printed in the newspaper. I have a horrible feeling that this has something to do with my father, and that someone bears him a grudge. I think they could have been getting at him through me.'

She gave an odd little shrug. 'I've asked my dad if he can think of anyone who has a grievance against him. He said he would think about it.' She fell silent, dwelling on all the other possibilities.

Rhys sent her a quick glance. 'I sense that there's something more going on in your head.'

'Well, of course, I may be wrong. There's always the possibility that I could be the target. The journalist hasn't exactly been friendly towards me, but I don't know how far he would take things. Maybe I should seek him out and ask him a question or two about that.'

'I don't think that would be a good idea.'

She looked at him. 'No? I disagree. I think it could well turn out to be the answer.'

Emma glanced out of the car window and saw that they were heading towards Docklands. She frowned. 'I thought you were going to take me home? This is certainly not the right way—I have to tell you, even in my wildest dreams I wouldn't have been able to afford to live in this area.'

He laughed. 'Possibly not… It just occurred to me that we might stop off at my place and get something to eat. You did say that you hadn't planned on going straight home, didn't you?'

'That's true.' She sent him a cautious glance.

'So is it all right if we go there? I thought you might like to look around. It's a beautiful warm day, and we could sit and eat on the terrace. Not that the food would be the great attraction—but I think I could whip up a quick paella. I know that used to be one of your favourites, and I generally tend to keep something of the sort stashed in the freezer.' He paused, and his dark brows came together momentarily. 'You wouldn't be expecting anything with fresh ingredients, would you?'

She chuckled, amused by his sudden doubts. 'That's all right. You may be an excellent doctor, and second to none on the emergency front, but I do know that cooking isn't one of your specialties. I wasn't exactly expecting you to provide me with food, but it sounds good.' He was making an effort to put things right, and she realised that she wasn't at all averse to the idea of going back to his apartment. In fact, she was intrigued to see where he lived.

His expression relaxed. 'That's settled, then. We're almost there.'

He drove into a secure underground parking space, and from there they took the lift to his penthouse apartment. Emma wasn't quite sure what she was expecting, but when he opened the door and gently ushered her inside, she found that she was unwittingly holding her breath.

They walked into a wide hallway, and from there he showed her into a huge reception room. At one end was a luxurious open-plan kitchen, with superbly modern appliances, all chrome and dark glass, and there was a utility room off to one side. Next to that, separated by an island bar, was the dining area. Beyond this was the great expanse of the living room, bordered along its length by floor-to-ceiling windows and glazed doors.

He opened up the doors and led her out onto the roof terrace. 'What do you think?' he asked.

She looked out at the stunning view of London and the Thames spread out before her, bathed in sunlight, the sky a beautiful pale blue.

She put a hand to her throat. 'It takes my breath away,' she said. 'I've never seen anything quite so lovely.'

He looked as though he was pleased by her reaction. 'Would you like to eat out here?'

She nodded. 'Yes, please. That would be good.' It was warm and sheltered there, and it was pleasing on the eye, with potted plants in abundance, adding bright splashes of colour.

'First, I'll show you the rest of the apartment, if you like.'

'Yes, please.'

The rest of the apartment was equally attractive. The bathroom was gleaming with ceramics and glassware, and the master bedroom was spacious, with French doors leading to its own balcony.

'Oh, how the other half live,' Emma said, as they went back to the kitchen. 'I can't believe that we're so far apart when it comes to lifestyles. What must you have thought of my tiny place?'

'I thought it was small and perfectly formed, just like its owner,' he murmured, a glint coming into his dark eyes.

'Yeah, right.' She gave him a doubtful look. Was he really saying that he thought she was attractive? Her mind did an odd little leap, but then she dismissed the thought. He was just playing with words, that was all.

Rhys started to rattle pots and pans, and she pulled herself together and went to help out with the preparations for the meal. It didn't take long. It was more a question of throwing ingredients into a pan and adding heat, and the microwave was a useful asset for everything else. Emma tossed salad and set things out on a tray, carrying what they needed through to the terrace.

Rhys opened a bottle of chilled wine. 'It's light,' he said, as he poured some into a glass for her, 'and it has a fruity taste. I think you'll like it.'

He was right. She did like it, perhaps a little too much. The food and the wine had a calming effect on her, helping to smooth away the rough edges of the day, so that after a while she felt languorous and completely at ease. When she had eaten her fill she leaned back in her chair and simply enjoyed the view.

'You're a better cook than you thought,' she murmured, sending him a lazy smile. 'That was delicious.'

'Sure I am,' he said, tongue in cheek. 'Just think of all the hours I spent preparing everything.'

She gave a soft laugh, but perhaps that was a mistake because it drew his glance to her mouth, and soon she became all too conscious of his gaze wandering slowly over her. Her blood began to race through her veins. Inside, her head was swirling, but that could have been the effect of the wine she had drunk.

Wasn't she setting herself up for danger by sitting here beside him, soaking up the balmy atmosphere? He was so close to her that she only had to reach out a hand to touch him, and she only had to say the word and he would kiss her, just as he had kissed her the day before. Wasn't that what she wanted?

A ringing started up in her ears, and at first she thought it was the wine, weaving a heady, intoxicating spell on her, but then Rhys flipped open his phone and the ringing stopped.

'No, I haven't seen her since this afternoon,' she heard him say. He glanced at his watch. 'That would be about three hours ago now, I guess. Perhaps she's gone to Elliot's place. Have you called his number?'

He waited, listening for a moment, and then said, 'All right, try not to worry. I'll ring around and perhaps I'll go over to her place and see if she's there. It might be that she's taking time out and isn't answering her phone for a while. I'll get back to you.'

He cut the call and glanced at Emma. 'That was my mother. Amy didn't meet them for tea as planned, and they're beginning to worry. Normally she would have called them to cancel.'

'Perhaps she's still with Elliot. It could be that they've made up and are spending some quiet time together.'

He shook his head. 'No, Elliot says she walked out on him and disappeared before he could catch up.' He grimaced. 'I'd better see what I can do to find her. In her state of mind, she might do something silly.'

'Is there anything I can do to help?'

'I don't think so. Besides, you probably have to get back to Kayla, don't you?'

'Yes, I do.' There wasn't any immediate hurry to do that. Tracey's mother was collecting the girls, but Emma sensed that he didn't want her tagging along. This was a family issue, and they were closing ranks. She wasn't wanted and, if the truth were known, she was part of the problem.

'I'll arrange a taxi for you,' Rhys said. Already he had withdrawn from her, his mind focussed only on his sister. That was how it should be, but Emma desperately wished that she could be included. Instead, she felt the cool chill of rejection settle around her.

CHAPTER EIGHT

'WHAT'S that noise?' Kayla stirred and rubbed her eyes, peering into the darkness.

Emma smoothed down the bed covers and tried to settle the little girl once more. 'It's just the wind making the leaves of the trees rustle,' she explained. 'Don't worry about it. Try to get some sleep. Think about all the fun you had at the party.'

Kayla smiled. 'We played chase on the pirate ship, and we hid in the tents.'

'You'll be able to tell Mummy all about it tomorrow, won't you?' Emma stroked the little girl's hair, soothing her, and waited until Kayla's eyelids began to droop. Once she saw that the child was sleeping, she slipped quietly out of the room.

She went and checked the security chain that Rhys had fitted, and then made sure that all the bolts were pushed home. Her nerves were beginning to fray at the edges. It wasn't the wind that Kayla had heard, she was sure of that.

Emma had been in bed when she'd first heard sounds

of scuffling, and when she had looked out of the window, staring out into the night, she had caught a glimpse of a shadowy figure. Someone had been prowling around outside, and Emma's spine had tingled in response. Her first thought had been to protect Kayla.

After what had happened to the dog, she didn't want to take any chances. Her phone was to hand, and at the first sign of anyone trying to get inside the house she would call the police.

After half an hour or so she went back to bed and huddled under the duvet, clutching it around herself as though it was a kind of protection from the outside world. She tried to get some sleep. She had to be on duty in the morning, and she needed to be fit for work.

Rhys gave her a long look when she arrived at their base some hours later. 'Are you feeling all right?' he asked.

'Yes, why do you ask?'

'You're very pale, and there are dark circles underneath your eyes. Are you sure that nothing's wrong?'

She decided to own up. 'I didn't get a lot of sleep. I thought someone was hanging about outside the flat. I can tell you, I was really glad of the security chain and the bolts. Even so, I think I was trying to listen for noises, just in case.' She made a grimace. 'Normally, I wouldn't have thought much about it, but after what happened to Samson I'm very much on my guard.'

'Didn't you tell the police about what happened to him? I would have thought they would make enquiries.'

She gave an awkward shrug. 'I didn't get around to

it—I've had such a hectic time of it lately, with one thing and another, and, anyway, I thought they might be too busy to check up on something like that. They would perhaps assume that he had got on someone's nerves with his barking and so on. I just wasn't sure that it was the right thing to do.'

'You don't think that putting poison down was a very strange thing for anyone to contemplate?' He gazed at her, an incredulous look in his eyes.

'Well, yes, of course I think that…I just wondered if they would take it as seriously as I did.'

He shook his head as though her logic was beyond him. 'How are you going to cope tonight? You can't let this situation go on, can you?'

'I'm taking Kayla over to my sister's house. She's having a get-together for her birthday, and we're going to have a sleep over. It'll be a bit cramped, but I'm sure it will turn out to be fun.'

A bleeping sound interrupted them, and James said, 'There's been an accident on an industrial estate. A spillage of chemicals at a factory, and several people are suffering from the effects of inhaling the vapours. We're supposed to put on protective clothing before we attend.'

They all sprang into action. As soon as they were kitted out, they ran to the helicopter, and when they were under way Emma asked Rhys, 'Did you manage to find Amy last night?'

'No…there's been no sign of her. She isn't at home, and Elliot hasn't seen her. I've tried the house, but I don't think she slept there last night. Apparently she and Elliot had a row after we left them.'

Emma winced. 'Perhaps she needed to get away for a clean break. It could be that she went to a hotel for the night.'

'I can't see why she would want to do that.'

'Perhaps you're worrying for no real reason. She's an adult after all, and she might have wanted to spend some time thinking things through without being disturbed.'

'There is that, I suppose. It's just that she's been through such a lot and, with her fragile state of mind lately, we're all worried about her. My parents are beside themselves. I'm going to have to go and look for her again, some time later on today. She isn't answering her phone.'

Emma frowned. 'Do you have any idea where to start?'

'No, but I suppose, as you say, I can at least check some of the local hotels. I'll have to give it some thought.'

The helicopter lurched as they began to make the descent towards the factory. 'What kind of chemical we dealing with?' Emma asked.

'It's a liquid used in the production of polyurethane polymers. It gives off noxious vapours. It's nasty stuff, and it acts as an irritant, so we can expect respiratory problems and skin reactions—maybe some gastric problems, too. We have to concentrate on getting people out of there as fast as possible, and above all we need to make sure that their airways are secure and deal with any breathing difficulties.'

Emma prepared herself for what awaited them. When they set down, it was apparent that everyone had already been brought out of the building. There were several ambulances in attendance, and the place was surrounded by police and fire crew.

Emma's first patient had stopped breathing, so she secured his airway and started CPR. When he took his first gasping breath, she gave him an injection of a bronchodilator and hurried with him to the helicopter.

A second patient was suffering from a spillage of the chemical on his arms. Martin found a source of water, and was gently running it over the man's skin. 'I'm going to keep doing this for quite a while,' he told the man. 'We'll probably be able to send you off to hospital in one of the ambulances.'

Rhys's patient was vomiting, and when he had rid his stomach of its contents, he began to wheeze. Swiftly, Rhys put in an airway and a nasogastric tube and made sure that he was receiving oxygen.

'OK, let's get these people to hospital,' he said. Within minutes, they were airborne once more.

Back at base, Emma expected that they would go out on another call, but Rhys instructed her to go and shower. 'Get rid of those outer clothes and all of your underthings,' he said. 'Put them into this bag and seal it, and stay under the water for at least ten minutes. I'll make sure that there are fresh clothes waiting for you.'

'You're going to sort out my underwear, are you?'

She gave him a sideways glance. 'Somehow I don't think so.'

'Let's have less of the lip,' he said. 'You'll be surprised what I can do. Go and get on with it.'

She didn't stay around to argue with him. Each member of the team went off to follow his orders, but Rhys was last to go and shower, making sure that everyone else followed instructions to the letter.

When she came out of the shower some time later, Emma was startled to find that he was as good as his word. A package of brand-new bra and briefs was waiting for her, along with a fresh medic's uniform. The uniform she could understand, but the underwear…? It was a perfect fit, and when she finally went back into the helicopter emergency unit, she gave Rhys an odd look.

He lifted a dark brow. 'You're wondering how I managed?' His mouth tilted. 'I had them flown in from Paris. Where they all right?'

'They were exactly right.' She viewed him with suspicion. Paris, of course, was pure fantasy. How had he actually managed it…and how was he so sure of her measurements?

He laughed at her uncertainty. 'I rang a local store,' he said, giving in, 'and had somebody bring them over. They were very obliging, and very quick, once I'd explained the predicament.' There was a gleam in his eyes as he looked her over. 'How did I do on size?'

'You did just fine,' she answered, heat coming into her cheeks, 'but I'm not sure I want to go into quite how you did that.'

His mouth curved, but by now the rest of the team was coming back into the room, and thankfully he dropped the subject.

'Are we going to hose down the helicopter?' Chris asked, as they gathered around some time later, drinking coffee and eating lunch. 'What about the interior?'

Rhys shook his head. 'Another crew is coming in to see to all that,' he said. 'I doubt that there is any real problem, and it's just a precaution, but we'll make sure that everything is done properly.'

'But what if there's a callout?' Emma wanted to know.

'We'll have to use the fast-response car. We don't have any other option.'

'Do these chemicals have any effects on the central nervous system?' Martin asked.

'It's possible. I'm hoping that most of the people we treated will come through this all right, but they'll probably need ongoing medical attention for some time. It's more likely that they'll suffer some kind of asthmatic problem in the future.'

Emma was frowning. 'Talking of ongoing problems,' she said, 'has there been any news about our car-crash victim? I wasn't really in any fit state to go and find out this morning.'

Rhys nodded. 'You made a good call there. They did a CT scan of her head and discovered a tumour in the membranes around the brain. It must have been growing for some time, and it was beginning to cause problems for her—headaches and dizziness, and some loss of memory.'

'So what's going to happen to her now?'

'They're going to start her on steroid drugs to reduce the swelling around the tumour, and then they're hoping to be able to operate. It all depends on whether they can do that without damaging any other structures within the brain. Either way, it seems that the crash has brought about a diagnosis.'

'I think maybe I'll go and check on her later,' Emma murmured. 'I just feel that I need to know how she's getting along. From what I heard, she has a young family. She struck a chord with me somehow.'

'Don't they all?' Rhys asked. He sent her a probing look, but there was amusement in his glance, and understanding, and she subsided, thinking about the pitfalls of this job they were trying to do. There were a lot of good sides to it, but the downside could be horrendous.

She didn't get a chance to follow up on Sarah's condition until her shift came to an end. Rhys walked with her to the A and E unit, and she wondered if he was going to leave her there and go his own way, but he suddenly appeared to change his mind about the whole thing. 'Wait, Emma. We should go back.' He touched her arm and tried to lead her back out into the corridor.

'What's wrong? I was going to find out what ward Sarah is on. I need to go back in there.'

'That's not good idea. Your reporter fellow is hanging around. He's probably checking up on the people we brought in from the factory this morning.' He grimaced. 'I think it would be for the best if you avoid him for the time being. You don't know if he's the one behind the poisoning, and you could set him off again simply by being around. I'll go in there and find out what you need to know.'

He started to urge her away from the unit, but Emma was having none of it. 'I'm not running away. I want to talk to him,' she said. 'I think I need to clear the air, one way or another.'

His mouth set in a resistant line. 'I think that would be a mistake.'

'Possibly, but I have to try.'

'Then I'll come with you.'

'No.' She shook her head. 'This is something that I need to do on my own.'

His eyes narrowed, and she thought he was going to object, so she hurried back into A and E, shrugging him off without giving him a chance to interfere. As she did so, she heard someone approach Rhys and engage him in conversation.

The reporter pounced as soon as he saw her. 'Ah, there you are, Dr Granger. I wondered if I might run into you. In fact, I was thinking of coming to find you.' He looked pleased with himself. 'I'm just asking about the people who were brought in here today from the industrial plant. You were there, at the factory, weren't you, treating them? People said the helicopter was called in. Do you have anything that you'd like to share with me?'

'Actually, yes...I do.' She sent him a cautious look. 'Although it has nothing to do with the incident this morning.'

'Oh?' He moved with her to the side of the room, obviously curious. 'What is it?'

'I wanted to ask you why you seem so intent on bringing up the past every time you write a story involving me. You know…bits about the restaurant, about the explosion and the accusations of negligence.'

She must have caught him unawares because he had the grace to look uncomfortable. Perhaps he hadn't expected her to come straight out with it. 'I was just telling the facts. People like to read stories that have a bit more depth. I thought it would be interesting to give them more detail about you, as you'd been in the news before.'

'So you were embellishing your story, and there was nothing personal I should read into it—is that what you're saying? The references you made to all the bad things that happened before didn't have anything to do with the fact that I wouldn't agree to go out with you?'

His expression wavered and he shifted, changing his stance a little as though she had caught him off guard. 'I'm not sure what you mean.'

'Then perhaps I should put it in a more straightforward way.' She looked him in the eyes, her gaze steady. 'Just after the explosion at the restaurant, you asked me out on a date, and I turned you down. I wondered if all this hostility I've been sensing from you has anything to do with that.'

'I don't…I mean, I didn't think about that.' He was faltering, searching for a way out of his predicament.

'You didn't?' She wasn't convinced. After all, as far

as she was aware, he had no other reason to pursue a vendetta against her, so she tried a new tack. 'Only, I hope you realise that when I turned you down, it wasn't because I had any problem with you—it was just that things were pretty awful back then. My head was in a terrible state. I couldn't think straight, and a friend of mine had been badly injured. My father lost his business. Perhaps I was short with you…and if so, I'm sorry for that. I didn't intend to be brusque.'

'I…um…' He was discomfited all over again, his gaze moving about the room as though he was searching for a way out.

She said, 'I didn't even know your name.' She glanced at his name badge. 'Jason…that has a nice ring to it.'

He stared at her and seemed to gather himself up. 'Does this mean that you might reconsider? I mean, would there be any chance…?'

'Of us going out on a date, you mean?' She wondered how she could let him down lightly. 'The trouble is, you see…I'm already involved with someone else.' It wasn't true, of course, unless you counted the fact that her heart had been tied up in knots for so long, hoping that Rhys would eventually come to realise that he wanted her in his life.

'Oh…so that's that, then.' He seemed disappointed. 'Are you sure?'

'I'm afraid so. I'm sorry.' She glanced back at the emergency room. 'You seem to be getting all the good stories, though. I suppose that might be some consolation.'

He appeared to be a little placated by that. 'My boss is holding a promotion out in front of my nose. I have to keep turning in good stories.' He frowned. 'I think perhaps I should get back to my interviews.'

'I won't keep you,' Emma said. She watched him walk away and hoped she had done the right thing in facing up to him, but when she returned to the corridor she was already beginning to have doubts. What if he took her attempt to pacify him the wrong way? Would he come to think that she had been patronising him?

'Are you quite mad?' Rhys said, coming over to her and taking hold of her arm. 'What were you thinking of?'

'You're still here,' she said, floundering. 'I thought you would have gone home by now.'

'I could hardly do that. I had to stay and make sure that you didn't land yourself in any more trouble, and I was just on my way to come and find you. I'd have come after you if your A and E consultant hadn't managed to waylay me in the corridor.'

'There was no trouble. He talked about how he's trying to get meaty copy for his paper.'

He sent her a laser-sharp stare. 'You took a big risk, facing up to him like that. You don't know what you're dealing with. Until you know the score, you should at least be a little more cautious.'

Emma was thoughtful. 'Yes, you could be right, but at least I feel a little more reassured now... I think he's harmless enough. Somehow, I don't think he's the one who has been following me.'

His mouth tightened. 'What am I going to do with

you? I'm beginning to think that you're more difficult to deal with than any of the patients.'

'Patients…' She sucked in a breath and glanced at her watch. 'That reminds me—I wonder if I still have time to go and look in on Sarah? I wanted to pay her a quick visit before I have to go and pick up Kayla.'

Rhys was frowning, looking at her in exasperation. 'I suppose it won't take too long, and I'll give you a lift home, so you won't have to negotiate the tube. I thought I would go and look for Amy, and your end of town seems a good place to start.'

'Actually,' she said, 'I've been thinking about that. When I was talking to Jason just now…' She broke off, seeing a look of disbelief come over Rhys's face. 'What's the matter? Did I say something wrong?'

'So you're calling him Jason now, are you? He wrecks your father's reputation, and all of a sudden you're on first-name terms with him.' His dark eyes held a piercing glint. 'I don't believe this. You must have taken leave of your senses.'

'And I suppose you and your family haven't been saying exactly the same thing about my father? Talk about the pot calling the kettle black.'

'That's hardly the same thing at all. None of us has broadcast our opinion to all and sundry.'

'Oh, no…so now you're saying your parents didn't try to put a stop to him opening his new restaurant?'

'That was a matter of health and safety. They felt they had to intervene in a quiet and subdued manner, so that people would ultimately be safe. Your journalist, on the other hand, has gone public with his judgements, painting a black and overly dramatic picture, and now you're stroking his ego. Next thing, you'll be telling me that you're going on a date with him.'

'No…I told him I couldn't do that because there was someone else.'

Rhys's eyes widened, and he took a step back, studying her as though she had slapped him in the face. 'You did?'

'Never mind all that. What I was going to say was I've been thinking about where Amy might be. I wonder if she would have thought of going back to the place where everything went wrong.'

He frowned and she said carefully, 'Sometimes, when people can't make sense of events, they go over and over things in their mind, and perhaps she decided to go back to the restaurant. After all, it was never pulled down. They secured it so that there was no danger to the public, but it was all shuttered and left. The insurance wouldn't pay out, and I think my dad couldn't face up to having it demolished. Perhaps he had some idea that one day he could start it up again.'

Rhys was deep in thought. 'You could be right, I suppose…but I don't know where she would have stayed last night. She might have found a place close by, so that she could go back there today. It could be worth going and taking a look.'

'I want to come with you this time,' she said, giving him an intent look. 'I need to be part of this… I can't explain it properly, but I feel that with all that's gone before I need to help to put things right…even though

I don't accept that my father was at fault… Do you understand?'

He nodded. 'Yes, I think I do. But what will you do about Kayla?'

'I'll see if Jane—Tracey's mother—will look after her for a little while longer. She's usually quite agreeable. She's been very good about things up to now, and the girls love playing together, so there shouldn't be any problem there.'

They went to look in on Sarah first of all. She was under sedation, and unable to move very easily because of the cast on her leg. The displacement of her hip had been corrected, but she was in a sorry state.

'Thank you for looking after me,' she said. She looked at Emma. 'The doctors told me that you had said there might be a problem—something that had made me crash. I suppose I'm glad that they found out what the trouble was, but I'm not sure I wanted to hear such bad news. I have to admit that I'm scared.'

'Anyone would be upset at hearing that kind of news,' Emma said, 'but at least now they know what caused your problems, the doctors can try to do something about it.'

Rhys added, 'If the surgeon decides to operate, there's a good chance that he can get the whole of the tumour out.'

Sarah's mouth trembled. 'What if he can't do that? What if it turns out to be malignant and they've caught it too late? How am I going to explain to my little boy and girl?'

'Let's not get ahead of ourselves. We don't know the full facts yet, and you should cross that bridge when you come to it,' Rhys said. 'If the worst happens, there are other ways of dealing with tumours…radiotherapy, for one, and chemotherapy.'

'I know. They tried to explain it to me, and I'm doing my best to be positive, but it's very hard.'

Emma patted her shoulder. 'It's bound to be difficult for you, but try to hold on, and keep talking to the doctors and nurses about any worries that you have.' Her eyes filled with compassion. 'Would it be all right if I came to see you again?'

'Yes, I'd like that.'

Emma was quiet as they made their way out of the hospital. She walked to the car with Rhys and he opened the passenger door for her, helping her into her seat. 'Buckle up,' he said.

'I do know what the procedure is,' Emma returned.

'Hmm…maybe, but I'm not sure what to make of you today. Perhaps it's just that you're overtired. You don't seem to be behaving in quite the same way as usual.'

He was probably still mulling over the fact that she had approached the reporter. It seemed to bother him for some reason, but she was too weary to work out why that should be.

'You're right,' she murmured. 'It's probably lack of sleep catching up with me—but I'm keyed up about seeing the old restaurant again. I haven't been back since the day it fell apart. It's something I have to do, but I think it's going to be difficult.'

They travelled across London until they arrived at the site of the crumpled building. It had been fenced off, and it was long overdue that it should have been pulled down, but there it was in all its faded glory. From the front, the building didn't look too bad, but Emma knew that it was around the back, in the old kitchen, where most of the damage remained.

'I'll see if I can find a way for us to get in,' Rhys said, parking up and going to stare at the front of the edifice. 'If I recall correctly, all of the doors have been boarded up, but there might be a window that we can reach.'

They were probably on a false errand, but Emma knew that there was no going back. Rhys knew it, too. This was the only other option that they could think of. Amy had been badly hurt because she had been in the restaurant, close to the kitchen door, when the explosion had occurred. Was it possible that she had come back to take a look at where it had all happened?

'There's a side door from the garage around the back,' Emma said, remembering. 'I don't think many people know about it. The garage door has never been particularly secure—maybe we should try to go in that way. The side door was kept locked, but I remember that we were having trouble with the key at the time. I don't know whether it was ever made good.'

Rhys climbed over the wooden fence that led into the garden of the old restaurant, and then stopped to help Emma to find a way over. He managed to free the garage door, and then he inspected the lock on the entrance to the main building.

'You're right,' he said. 'It hasn't been closed properly. We should be able to get inside easily enough.'

Emma took a tentative step inside the building. She hadn't been sure how she would feel, coming back to this place, but already the breath was catching in her lungs, and it was as though she could smell the soot from the fire. It seemed to hang in the air. She realised that her heart was hammering.

Rhys must have guessed how she was feeling. He put an arm around her, supporting her, holding her close, so that his warmth gave her strength, and all at once she found her courage starting to seep back. He looked at her. 'Are you ready to go on?'

She nodded. They began to walk through what was left of the kitchen, picking their way over fallen masonry, and suddenly she came to a halt and looked around, her glance going over the damaged cooking range and the dented metal cabinets.

'What is it?' Rhys asked.

'There was no gas cylinder in here,' she said. 'It's just occurred to me. I'd been talking to Amy and the chef in the restaurant, and someone came up with a great idea for a fruit starter, and we were all adding silly notions to the recipe. We were laughing, and I went into the kitchen, looking for my dad. I wanted to tell him about it, but he was chatting with somebody at a table outside in the garden, near the barbecue. I stayed out there with him for a few minutes, and it was then that we heard the explosion.' She pressed her lips together as the enormity of her recovered memory came back to her. 'My father never set foot in the kitchen in that time. He certainly didn't get the cylinder out or ask anyone else to do it.'

'You're saying that someone came in and set up the cylinder during those few minutes when the kitchen was empty?'

'Yes, that's what I'm saying. I've only just thought about it, but I remember looking around, because I wanted to see if any of the lower cabinets were open. We kept some of the desserts in there because they were cool.' She looked at him. 'How could I have forgotten that?'

'Memory is a strange thing,' he said. 'I imagine the horror of the day must have blotted it out.'

They made their way over rubble and broken beams into the restaurant. Emma stared around her and drew in a quick, sharp breath. Rhys gave her a hug, and glanced at her as though asking if she would be all right.

'I'm OK,' she said, and then he left her, his gaze following the direction of her transfixed stare. He walked over to a figure that was huddled in a corner of the room.

'Amy,' he said softly, kneeling down beside his sister, 'I thought we'd lost you, but you're safe now. I've got you.'

Amy looked up at him. Her face was streaked with dirt and dried tears, but beneath the dust she was pale and cold. He took off his jacket and covered her with it, and then he sat down next to her and held her in his arms. He stroked her hair, cradling her head against his chest.

She started to cry, and he said softly, 'It's all right. It's going to be all right from now on.'

He glanced up at Emma, and she drew out her mobile phone and looked at him questioningly. 'Call my parents,' he said in a low tone, giving her the number.

She went outside and made the call, and then she went back to the restaurant to see if there was anything she could do to help. It looked as though Amy might have been there all night. She was shivering now, and Rhys gently rubbed her arms, trying to get warmth back into his sister's limbs.

'I think she's dehydrated,' Rhys said. 'There's probably a bottle of something in my car—juice or a glucose drink, or some such.' He tossed the keys to Emma. 'Would you mind getting it for me? There should be a blanket in the boot as well.'

She hurried away to fetch what was needed. When she went back into the restaurant, Rhys covered his sister with the blanket and then helped her to sip the drink, holding the bottle steady for her.

'Your parents are coming over,' Emma said. 'I tried to tell them that we would bring her to them, but they didn't want to wait. They felt that they had to come to her right now. I'll see if I can get the front door open for them. It shouldn't be too difficult to pull the boards away.'

He nodded, and Emma went to try to free up the door. By the time she had finished, Rhys had managed to coax a few words out of his sister.

'I let Elliot down,' Amy said, her voice still a little croaky from the dust. 'He wanted a family so much. I thought we were going to be so happy together, and it all went wrong when I lost the baby.'

Emma was afraid that if she said anything Amy would retreat back into her shell, but it bothered her that Amy should feel that there was no hope.

'You managed to conceive once,' she murmured. 'That means that there is always a chance that you'll do so again. It might even happen without medical intervention, because once the body has been turned on to pregnancy, it sometimes happens that things proceed normally.'

Amy looked at her. 'It's not going to happen for us,' she said in a broken voice. 'Elliot doesn't want me any more. He doesn't find me attractive. He didn't want to touch me once I got home from the hospital. I can't blame him for that. I can't really blame him for looking elsewhere.'

'He didn't look elsewhere,' Emma said. 'I'm sure that he loves you very much. Perhaps he was simply afraid that you were hurting so much after your operation. You just need to be able to talk things through with him. I mean, talk to him properly. You have to tell him how you've been feeling, about all the things that bother you.'

She wanted to say more, but Amy's parents arrived just then, and she showed them through to where Amy was still huddled in a corner with Rhys.

'She's all right. It's just that she's been here all night, and she's cold and dehydrated. She's upset, of course.'

Amy's mother looked at her. 'She's been upset for a long time.' She hurried over to her daughter.

Her husband stopped to glance back at Emma. 'This place should have been pulled down long ago,' he said.

'Is there anything I can do to help?' Emma said, going over to the small group.

She saw that Amy's hands were cut and streaked with dried blood, and she guessed that she had tried to break down the fence in order to get in. It would have been awkward for her to climb, given that her hip was somewhat stiff. Her problems weren't going to be easily resolved. Rhys's sister would need expert counselling.

'Do you want me to arrange for her to be seen by someone at the hospital?'

'I think we'll leave that,' Rhys said. 'Perhaps her own doctor can take a look at her later.'

'We'll manage,' Amy's mother said. 'She'll be all right with us.'

'We should probably get Elliot to come over to our place,' her father said. 'Maybe it would help if he was to talk to her.'

Emma looked at the family gathered around Amy. They had turned away from Emma, and seemed to be excluding her. They were giving all of their attention to Amy, and that was to be expected. It was perfectly natural and it was good, but Emma suddenly felt as though they had put up a defensive wall around her, and Emma was on the other side of that wall. She was an outsider and the family group was forbidden territory.

She took a step backwards. She wanted to say something, but the words stuck in her throat. Rhys had his back to her, and he was busy tending to his sister.

Emma quietly moved away. She went out of the front

door, and gently pulled it closed behind her. She didn't belong here. She had no part to play in Rhys's life. It was surely time she became used to that idea.

CHAPTER NINE

'IT's good to see you looking so much better, Lindsey,' Emma said with a smile. 'Are you sure all the arrangements have been made for getting you home? Is there anything you need me to do?'

'No, thanks, everything's sorted. My parents are back from their holiday and they're coming to fetch me and take me to their place so that I can recuperate. We'll pick up Kayla from nursery school on the way...and Samson from the vet, all being well. Apparently he's very nearly back to normal, and he's beginning to demand lots of attention. He wants the nurses to play with him all the time.'

Emma's mouth curved. 'I can imagine. He obviously misses you and Kayla. She always manages to keep him occupied.'

'That's very true.'

'Actually, I called in at the vet's on the way here, to see how Samson was doing, and I could see for myself that he was absolutely fine. They said he'd definitely be able to come home with you today. And that he was in very good form, completely back to normal.'

Emma smiled, seeing Lindsey's obvious relief. 'You'll have to go on giving him medication for a little while longer, but that's only as a precaution, to prevent any possibility of a relapse. They always recommend that there's follow-up treatment for a week or so after this kind of illness, because it ensures that he won't suffer any ongoing effects. They told me he's back to his former good health, as if this had never happened.'

'I'm so pleased.' Lindsey reached for Emma's hand and squeezed it gently. 'Thanks for taking care of everything for me while I've been stuck in here, Emma. You've been a good friend, the best.'

'I'm just glad to see you on the mend.' Emma glanced at the clock on the wall. 'I must go. I'm still on duty, and I just grabbed a few minutes to come and see you while James refuels the helicopter. He'll be back any time now.'

She hurried to the air ambulance headquarters, and readied herself for work once more, psyching herself up to face Rhys. So far, the atmosphere between them had been somewhat strained and she had a feeling of treading on eggshells around him.

For herself, she was still coming to terms with the finality of never again being welcomed into his family, while he had been in an odd sort of mood all day, hardly saying a word to anyone. So far, she hadn't been able to completely fathom his mind-set, but she guessed that he must be very worried about his sister.

He was sorting out his medical kit when she walked into the base, and she went to do likewise with her own, refreshing supplies.

'I've just been to see Lindsey,' she told him. 'She's being discharged from hospital today.'

'I guessed that she might be any time now. I suppose you'll still be keeping an eye on her for the time being,' he said, tucking a set of dressings into his bag.

'When she's home, for a while, yes, I dare say, but her husband is on his way back to the UK, and she'll be staying with her parents tonight.' She glanced at him. 'It's good when the family gathers around, isn't it? I noticed that with Amy. She was vulnerable, but she was drawn into a protective circle by you and your parents, and that was something very precious to see.'

'Was it? I wasn't aware that you stayed around for long enough to see what was going on.' His gaze flitted over her. 'I looked for you, and you had disappeared…but, then, I expect you had other things to do. You had to get back home for Kayla, didn't you?'

'That's right.' She wasn't going to tell him the real reason that she had left so suddenly. 'You were all busy and I thought it best to slip away. There wasn't anything more I could do.'

'No, probably not.' He stopped what he was doing and studied her for a long moment. He said on a cautious note, as though it was difficult for him to put it into words, 'I should have said this before now, but we owe you far more than we can say for helping us to find Amy. I don't think we would have thought to go back to the restaurant to look for her.'

'I think you would have, given time. It's just that it's often uppermost in my mind, for obvious reasons.' She wondered why it had been hard for him to say that, but she covered her misgivings by rummaging around for fresh syringes.

She wondered how Amy was coping now. 'You said earlier that Amy was a lot better in herself once she was home and cosseted. Did she get to see Elliot? I can't help thinking that he's somehow at the root of all her troubles. I know the accident was the spark that set things off, but I'm wondering if he is the key to everything.'

'I'm not sure of his role in all this, but he said he was going to spend some time with her today. She's staying at my parents' house for the time being, but they'll make room for Elliot, too, if need be.'

'That's good.'

At least Rhys was a bit more forthcoming now, but he was still faintly reserved in his manner towards her and she would have liked to know what was on his mind. Perhaps he had expected her to lend more support. He was clearly alarmed by the way Amy had taken off, and it might be that he was afraid she was heading for a complete breakdown.

She didn't get the chance to ask him about that, though, because they were interrupted by a sudden callout to a road traffic accident.

'It isn't the usual thing,' Rhys said, coming back to Emma and Martin with the details. 'Apparently a woman was bringing in her little girl to the hospital, but she's stuck in traffic because of an accident further along the road. She called the emergency services to say that she's worried about the little girl's condition and it appears that we need to get to her as fast as we can. The ambulance crew can't get to her, but they sent a paramedic.'

They scrambled to the helicopter, and set down a few minutes later on a grassed area close to where the traffic was gridlocked. Emma hurried over to the little girl, and she could see straight away that she was in a pitiful condition. The child wasn't much more than three years old. She was lethargic in her mother's arms, and her lips had a bluish tinge. The paramedic was checking her vital signs.

'She's feverish,' Emma told Rhys, after she had made a quick examination. 'Her breathing is fast, and she has a tachycardia—the heart rate is way faster than it should be. Her blood pressure is very low and she's going into shock.'

'Please, do something for her,' the child's mother begged. 'I've never seen Molly like this before. Please help her.'

'I promise you, we'll do everything that we can,' Rhys murmured, checking the little girl's blood oxygen levels with a pulse oximeter. 'It's clear that she's very ill. Has she has any infections lately, any sign that she was unwell before this?'

Emma could see that he was concerned for the child. His grey eyes darkened as he looked down at her, and she sensed that Molly's vulnerability touched him and affected him deeply.

Watching him, it occurred to her that he would make

a good and very caring father, and her heart gave an odd little lurch. It was almost painful to know that she would never have the chance to be the mother of his children.

'She had a cough,' the woman said. 'My GP didn't think there was too much wrong with her. He said it was a virus, and it should resolve itself. I tried giving her some cough medicine, but it didn't seem to do any good, and she just started to get worse. I was going to take her back to the doctor, but the surgery was closed and everyone was out on call. She seemed to be going downhill very fast. I thought if I drove her to the hospital…'

'You did everything you could,' Rhys said. 'You couldn't have done any more.'

Martin was already giving the little girl oxygen through a mask, but Emma said, 'I think we need to intubate her to secure her airway.'

Rhys nodded. 'You do that, while I try to gain intravenous access.' He turned to the mother. 'I'm going to take a sample of Molly's blood for testing. We'll need to do blood cultures to see if we're dealing with some kind of bacterial infection but, rather than wait for the results, I'm going to start her on antibiotic therapy straight away.'

They took the child and her mother into the helicopter and soon they were on their way to the hospital. 'It looks like sepsis,' Rhys said, glancing at Emma. 'Her body is overloaded with toxins. With the lung involvement, it's probably pneumonia, but the tests will give us the answer.'

Emma was desperately worried about the little girl. She supervised the child's transfer to the medical team at the hospital, and had to accept that now Molly was in their hands.

Then she realised with a sense of anticlimax that her shift had come to an end, and her spirits went into a downwards spiral. That was the trouble with this job. One minute her adrenaline was running high, and then she was tossed down to ground level with a bump. She wanted to know what was happening with the little girl, but she knew there would be no news for some time.

Rhys was busy going over the day's events with James, carefully logging everything onto the computer. Emma slipped away, leaving them to it, but she didn't go straight home. Instead, she went to call in on Sarah, the woman with the newly diagnosed brain tumour. She wanted to know if there had been any developments. This, at least, was one case where she could follow up.

'They say that they'll do the operation tomorrow,' Sarah told her. She looked more comfortable now that the healing process was beginning. 'They've done more tests, and it's looking as though it should be fairly easy to remove the tumour. It's not attached to any other vital structures, as far as they can see, so the only worry is whether it's malignant or not. If they can remove it all, they seem to think that I'll be fine from then on.'

'That's really good news,' Emma said. 'I believe most of these kinds of tumours are benign, so we'll keep our fingers crossed for you.'

'Thanks.'

Sarah looked more positive than she had done for some time, and Emma left her, telling her that she would come back and see her after the operation. By then they would have done the biopsy and she would know whether the news was good or bad.

It seemed strange to be going home to an empty flat. This last week, looking after Kayla, she had grown used to having somebody about the place. It had made up in part for not having Lindsey next door, but now she felt strangely isolated.

Someone walked by the alleyway at the back of the house as she approached her front door. It was a man wearing a jacket very much like the one that Rhys sometimes wore, and she called out, 'Rhys…is that you?' But no one came in answer to her query. Sighing, she put the key in her lock and went inside. Perhaps she was beginning to imagine things.

More than anything, she would have liked Rhys to be somewhere near by. It was one thing to work with him, but she missed the closeness, the way he had comforted her, put his arms around her and drawn her against his chest. She had grown to love him, she recognised that all too clearly now, and it hurt that he couldn't love her in return.

She went through the motions of cleaning the flat, of tidying up and putting everything in its place. It was still a warm day, although it was drawing to a close, and she pushed open the French doors so that she could go out into the courtyard to water the plants and let some fresh air into the house.

Going back inside, she put the watering-can away in the cupboard and thought about preparing some supper. A noise disturbed her, a crunching sound, like gravel being trampled underfoot, and she frowned and went to peer out of the window at the front of the house. No one was there, and she went back to the kitchen to get on with collecting together the ingredients for a light salad. She was hyped up, that was the problem. Everything was a let down after the tension of being at work.

She lost herself in daydreams. Would Rhys invite her back to his apartment some day? There had been something special about the meal they prepared together. They had laughed and teased one another about the ingredients, and when they had at last sat down to eat, the sun had been warm on her skin, and his smile had lit her up inside.

Another sound broke into her reverie. This time it was a dull thud, and it seemed to be coming from next door, which was odd because Lindsey wasn't there. Her flat was empty.

Her pulse quickened. Was she getting worked up over nothing? Even so, she reached for her phone and dialled Rhys's number, just for the comfort of hearing him speak.

There was no answer, and disappointment washed over her as the call switched to voicemail. She started to leave a message for him.

'Rhys…I just wanted to say…' She broke off. It was too difficult to tell him that she needed him and wanted him to be there with her. 'I hope Amy's feeling better.

I'm sure things will work out for her if she gives Elliot a chance.'

She cut the call. Going back to her salad, she washed lettuce under the tap, and then put it into a shaker to dry it out.

'Well, isn't that a familiar scene?' a man's voice droned. 'Here you are preparing a meal…a few lettuce leaves here, radish, a sprinkling of onion, some nuts and peppers, a light salad dressing. It's something you do every day, isn't it, without giving it much thought?'

Emma turned around. She didn't recognise the voice, and when she looked at the man who was standing there, just a few yards away from her, in her kitchen, she wasn't at all sure whether she had ever seen him before. She felt cold all over.

'Who are you? What are you doing here?' She stared at him. He was of medium build, with dark straggly hair that flopped down across his forehead and lay in unkempt strands over his collar. 'How did you get in?' she asked.

He didn't answer her, and her throat started to dry up, her heart beginning to thud heavily against her rib cage. Was this the person who had tried to poison Lindsey's dog? What was he doing there, in her kitchen?

She glanced towards the end of the room, and saw that the French windows had been pulled together. They weren't closed, just drawn inwards, as though to keep out any noise.

'You came in through the courtyard, didn't you?' she said. 'Why are you here? What is it that you want with me?'

'Well, now, there's the thing…what is it that I want?' His mouth pursed as though he was thinking, and his eyes closed to small dark slits. He came towards her. 'I suppose I want my life back.' He scowled at her. 'You took it from me.'

She frowned. 'How did I do that?'

His lips made an ugly shape. 'You don't remember, do you? You and your family—you walk all over everyone. You think you can have it all, and you don't care who gets in your way.' He looked at the food that she was preparing, and she wondered if she ought to stand in front of the knife that she had been using to cut the vegetables. Perhaps it would be best to keep temptation out of his way. She moved a little to one side.

'I used to prepare food every day,' he said. 'It was good food, people used to say how tasty it was.'

Emma stared at him. This man had never worked in her father's kitchens, that she knew for sure, but she was beginning to feel that she had seen him somewhere before. Another restaurant, was that it?

Recognition dawned at last. She said slowly, 'You had the restaurant on the other side of the square, didn't you? I remember you did good business over there.'

'Until you and your father came along.' His lips twisted in an ugly sneer. 'It was bad enough that he started up in opposition to me, but then you had to come along with your big ideas. Barbecues and themed events… You had it all worked out, didn't you? Anything to draw in a crowd and take the customers away from me. I lost my livelihood because of you and your father.'

She frowned, trying to take it all in. He hated her so much, but surely she hadn't done anything to hurt him? 'You had lots of customers,' she said. 'We didn't take anything away from you.'

'They closed me down...the environmental people. Food poisoning, they said. It was all your fault. You sent them.' He made a grimace that was meant to be a smile. 'I got my own back. I poisoned your dog. He was very partial to a bit of meat, wasn't he?'

Emma's head was reeling. Her fears had been right all along, and that meant this man was capable of anything. 'I didn't do anything,' she said in a strained voice. 'I certainly didn't send the health inspectors your way.' A thought occurred to her. 'Was it you who was responsible for blowing up the kitchen?'

He laughed, a harsh, cracking sound that echoed through the room. 'Good, wasn't it? I thought that would close things down, and it did.'

Emma felt faint all of a sudden. This man was dangerous, and she was trapped in her own home with him, with no one to call on for help. Did he have a concealed weapon somewhere about him? How was she going to protect herself?

She said heavily, 'Didn't you care that you might have killed innocent people?'

'Most of them were outside near the barbecue, and the kitchen was empty. I knew if I destroyed the kitchen I would put an end to the business. It wasn't difficult. I knew where the gas cylinders were kept.'

She wanted to be sick. He started towards her and her

body tensed. She couldn't think what to do, but as he came within touching distance of her she reached for the water filter and tipped it over him, drenching him with cold water. He spluttered, shocked by her unexpected action, but it gave her the seconds she needed to head for the French doors.

They were wide open, and as she took that fact in she realised that she was not alone with the man. Rhys was sprinting towards him, and while her would-be attacker was still recovering from the effects of his cold shower, Rhys grappled him face down on to the ground and held him in an arm lock.

'I need a belt, or something to tie him with,' Rhys muttered, and she whipped the thin leather belt from around the waist of her jeans and handed it to him. Her hands were shaking.

'I can't believe that you're here,' she said, her breath coming in short spurts. 'I've never been so relieved to see anyone in my life.'

He managed a wry smile. 'Me, too. I wouldn't like to think what might have happened if I hadn't decided to come over here.' He was holding the man down with his body, his knees pressed into his back, and it came to Emma that she ought to be helping out.

'I'll call the police,' she said, but he stopped her with a shake of his head.

'There's no need. I already called them and they're on their way.'

'They are?'

'That's right.' He looked at her and smiled, and it

was as though the sun had come out. 'I didn't want to leave you here on your own for another night, not after what you told me about hearing somebody prowling around. I knew that you would be all right last night, because you said that you were going to stay with your sister. I felt I had to come and make sure that you were safe.'

A little glow started up inside her. She went and knelt down beside him, needing to be close to him all at once. 'I rang you, but I thought you were busy. I just wanted to talk to you—to hear your voice.'

'Did you? I haven't checked my phone yet, so I didn't know that. I phoned Amy earlier, to see how she was doing, and it looks as though she and Elliot have managed to patch things up, but apart from that I haven't checked any of my messages. I came straight over here once I had finished at the hospital. I was a little late because I went to check on the child with pneumonia. She's showing signs of responding to the antibiotics…nothing too spectacular as yet, but enough to give us hope.'

'I'm glad about that.' She gazed up at him. 'So you came here especially to make sure that I was all right?'

He nodded. 'As soon as I got here, I thought I saw someone hanging around. He was acting suspiciously, so I followed him.'

Emma frowned. 'Are you saying that you've been here for some time—why didn't you intervene before this?'

He reached into his pocket and pulled out his phone,

flipping it open. 'Because I was trying to capture it on the videophone. The police will want some evidence, and I think we have him pretty well tied up…not just for today's events but for everything that has gone before…don't you agree?'

He played back some of the footage of the trespasser in her kitchen, and the voice on it told its own tale. 'Oh, yes, I see what you mean.' She smiled at him. 'I'm so glad that you're here.'

It wasn't long after that before the police were knocking at the door, and Rhys handed over both the man and the phone into their custody. 'I think perhaps he should see not just the police surgeon but a psychiatrist,' he told the officers. 'I believe he has some serious mental problems.'

'We'll mention it to the doctor on duty,' the arresting officer said.

Emma saw them out, and then went back into her living room. She pulled in a deep breath. 'I'm so relieved that's all over.'

'So am I.' Rhys put his arms around her, gathering her up, and she went into his embrace, feeling that for once the world was spinning properly on its axis.

'I wasn't sure what I was going to do,' she murmured, her words muffled against his chest. 'I was so afraid, and I kept thinking, How am I going to get him out of here? Knowing what he was capable of was terrifying.'

'I thought you managed the situation really well, by keeping him talking,' Rhys said, leading her over to the settee and drawing her down beside him onto the soft cushions. 'I was getting ready to step in at any moment, but it occurred to me that I ought to record what he was saying. It's the only proof we have…unless they search his place and find rat poison, of course. Even then, they have to associate his actions with what happened to Samson. I'm not sure what evidence they could find to connect him with the gas cylinder, but now that we have a suspect, it might serve to jog someone's memory. Someone might recall seeing him at the restaurant.'

Emma shuddered. 'It feels as though I've been working my way through one long nightmare,' she said. 'Is it finally over?'

He stroked her hair, his other arm circling her and keeping her close to him. Her whole body warmed at his touch. It felt so good to be near to him, to have him fold her against him this way. 'It's over,' he said. 'Only perhaps another dream is just beginning…'

She looked up at him. 'Is it? What do you mean?'

'I mean that I want to be able to keep you safe from now on. I can't go through this again. I need to know that you aren't going to come to any harm, and the only way that I can do that is to keep a very close eye on you. I think I need to make you part of my life…a very essential, precious part of my life.'

Her eyes widened. 'That sounds like… almost like a proposal of some kind. I'm not sure that I understand what you're saying.' Did he really want to keep her close by him? Dared she hope that his feelings for her were something extra-special?

His mouth made a rueful slant. 'I don't think I've ever been able to express myself properly where you're concerned, Emma. You mean so much to me, and I've always had to hold back, to try to keep my feelings to myself.'

'You have?' Her brows drew together. 'Why?'

He ran a finger lightly along her hairline, pausing to trace a path along her cheekbone. He said softly, 'Because it wouldn't have been fair of me to tell you how I felt about you. You were so young when we first met, and you were full of life, ready to go out into the world and full of plans to become a doctor. I couldn't hold you back, but I was jealous of everyone who came into your life. You had no experience of men at all, and I knew I had to let you go free to spread your wings.'

His voice rasped in his throat. 'It tore me apart to do that. I was so afraid that you would take up with some man who would whisk you away and then I would never have the chance to tell you how much I love you, and that I want you only for myself.'

'You love me?' she said. 'Did you just say that you love me?'

He looked into her eyes. 'I did. I said it. I love you.' He bent his head and kissed her, trailing fire along her lips, as though he would seal his love for her with the imprint of his mouth on hers.

Her world tilted as the blood rushed to her head and her mind started to spin. Was he really saying what she had yearned to hear for so long? Had that kiss been a signal that all her dreams were about to come true?

She said huskily, 'Why did you wait so long to tell me? Didn't you know that was what I wanted to hear?'

'Did you?' He smiled into her eyes and kissed her again, tugging her close to him, his hands stroking her, smoothing along the length of her spine and coming to settle on the rounded curve of her hip. 'You were always so wary of me, so guarded in the way you approached me. I thought perhaps you were still striving for your independence, that you didn't want to work with me, let alone be landed with me as your boss.'

She shook her head. 'It wasn't like that at all. I wanted you so much, but I thought your family was against me…against my father…and I felt helpless. No one would listen when I tried to defend him. Your parents seemed to shut me out…they wanted to stop my father from starting up again. There were so many reasons why our relationship wouldn't work.'

Her eyes clouded. 'You went along with them. You blamed my father for what happened to Amy and you even believed that I would try to steal her husband. How could you even think like that?'

'I didn't know then what the truth was regarding your father, but I certainly didn't blame you for any sins that might be his. My parents weren't sure about his role, but they felt they had to do what was right and above all they had to be loyal to Amy. She was their priority. They were worried to death when they found her in the restaurant yesterday, and they know that they were short with you and offhand. They told me that they're sorry for that. After they had time to think things through, they realised that they were being unfair.'

Rhys pressed his lips together in a thoughtful manner. 'Amy and Elliot talked things through earlier today. Apparently, ever since the accident, she felt that she was unattractive, especially because of the limp—which is actually hardly noticeable. She convinced herself that Elliot didn't want her any more.' He shook his head. 'It's strange how the mind can delude itself, isn't it?'

His gaze meshed with hers. 'None of this was ever your fault. We all know that you did whatever you could to help her. In the end, you were the one who found her, back at the restaurant, and we owe you a debt of gratitude for that.'

Emma tugged at her lower lip with her teeth. 'I'm glad they managed to see things from my point of view after all. It doesn't alter the fact that you were cool towards me, though. I was friendly with Elliot, but you treated me as though I was betraying your sister. I could understand Amy feeling that way, because she was depressed and obviously not thinking straight, but how could you do that?'

He gave a ragged sigh. 'I told myself that Elliot was the problem, but he wasn't. It was just that I was desperate to be with you, to have you all to myself. More than anything, I needed to hold you and kiss you and show you exactly how I felt about you. Perhaps I grasped at the chance to use Elliot as an excuse…'

He cupped her face with his hand, his thumb stroking the softness of her cheek. 'It was so hard for me to be around you, feeling the way I do, and to have to keep my distance. I was struggling to stay in control of myself. We had to work together and it was unbelievably difficult for me to act as though we were simply colleagues, when all I wanted to do was to hold you close and show you how much I care.'

Emma lifted a hand to cover his. She snuggled her cheek against his palm, loving the way he was touching her. It made her feel cherished, as though she was the most precious thing in the world to him. 'Didn't you know how much I wanted you, too?'

The breath caught in his throat. 'That makes me feel so good. All I wanted was to show you that I could make you happy if only you would give me the chance. I hoped that you would choose me—no one else just me.'

He kissed her gently, and as her lips parted and softened against his, she could feel the heavy thud of his heartbeat pounding in unison with her own.

He said huskily, 'As to that reporter...I hated the thought of him being able to get close to you. The prospect of him taking you out on a date was altogether too much.'

She gave a soft laugh. 'As if he would ever get the chance. You are a fool, Rhys.'

'I know. Can you forgive me?'

His expression was abject, and she melted instantly. 'I'll forgive you anything. I love you. I've always loved you. That was why I had no experience of other men. You were the only one for me, and I didn't want to spread my wings. I wanted to stay with you and have you tell me that I was the only woman in your life, but you never did that.'

'I'll make up for it now. You are the only woman in my life, Emma. Will you marry me? Will you stay by my side for now and for always?'

She saw all the love and need expressed in the depths of his grey eyes. 'I will,' she murmured.

She smiled up at him, and that was all the invitation he needed. His arms closed around her, wrapping her in his embrace, and he kissed her tenderly, drawing her down into the sweet, honeyed cocoon of a love that would last for a lifetime.

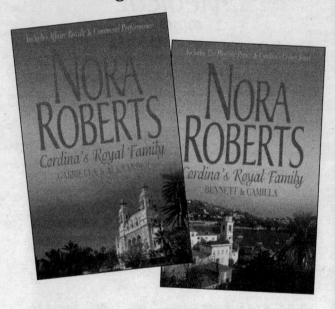

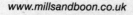

FREE

4 BOOKS AND A SURPRISE GIFT!

We would like to take this opportunity to thank you for reading this Mills & Boon® book by offering you the chance to take FOUR more specially selected titles from the Medical Romance™ series absolutely FREE! We're also making this offer to introduce you to the benefits of the Mills & Boon® Reader Service™—

- ★ **FREE home delivery**
- ★ **FREE gifts and competitions**
- ★ **FREE monthly Newsletter**
- ★ **Books available before they're in the shops**
- ★ **Exclusive Reader Service offers**

Accepting these FREE books and gift places you under no obligation to buy; you may cancel at any time, even after receiving your free shipment. Simply complete your details below and return the entire page to the address below. You don't even need a stamp!

YES! Please send me 4 free Medical Romance books and a surprise gift. I understand that unless you hear from me, I will receive 6 superb new titles every month for just £2.80 each, postage and packing free. I am under no obligation to purchase any books and may cancel my subscription at any time. The free books and gift will be mine to keep in any case.

M7ZEE

Ms/Mrs/Miss/Mr..Initials ....
BLOCK CAPITALS PLEASE

Surname ....

Address ....

....

....Postcode ....

Send this whole page to:
The Reader Service, FREEPOST CN81, Croydon, CR9 3WZ